Anne H. Oman

MANGO RAINS

To Elizabeth Becker,
who wrote The
sequel,
With thanks,
Anne Oman

Mango Rains

ANNE H. OMAN

"Happiness makes up in height for what it lacks in length."

Robert Frost

ANNE H. OMAN

Part 1: Phnom Penh, 1963

ANNE H. OMAN

Namaste

Before the monsoon came the mango rains, which were short, hard downpours that forced the mango trees to surrender their just-ripe fruits and tantalized the city's inhabitants with a hint of the release the monsoon rains would soon bring. Julia Galbraith, a newly arrived Foreign Service Officer, just short of her twenty-third birthday, stood on the terrace of her ground-floor apartment on the rue Pasteur and watched the rain fall. She was not beautiful, or even pretty, but she was tall and slender and blonde, which almost made up for that lack. Though a little shy, she exuded the freshness and vulnerability of a woman on the brink of life.

Soon the torrent ceased as abruptly as it began, and the steam rose from the earth and the pavement, leaving the downed frangipani blossoms on the sidewalk as the only evidence that it had rained at all. The people who always clustered on the curb outside the building – the soup sellers with their kerosene stoves whose smoke floated languidly in the humid air, the fruit vendors with their heavily laden carts and the *cyclo-pousse* drivers with the black-and-white scarves tied around their heads to catch the sweat – emerged from the temporary shelter of the towering tamarind trees, and the pace of the street resumed. The downed blossoms were quickly trampled underfoot, their furled white petals soiled and broken like bruised flesh.

The French-colonial apartment building, circa 1920, was set back from the street and surrounded by lush foliage, which along with the overhead fans and the 12-foot ceilings and the marble floors kept the apartment reasonably cool. The sole air conditioner was in the bedroom, and Julia used it only occasionally when it rained so hard that the tall shutters had to be closed. The cavernous living room was sparsely furnished with sagging rattan furniture, whose well-worn cushions testified to several generations of previous sitters. The dining room had a long table, where she ate most of her meals in solitary splendor, and a buffet where she placed the formal invitations to receptions and dinners that even a junior officer received. The Embassy Security Officer had told everyone to do this so that if the Cambodian police came searching for them, the servants would be able to produce the invitations and escape harassment. Julia had scoffed at the idea that anyone would care about her whereabouts, but the buffet was a handy place to leave such things – and doing so made life seem more exciting and dangerous than it really was. Next to the dining room was a small service kitchen with only a refrigerator and a sink. The actual cooking was done across a passageway by Lanh, her Vietnamese *boyesse*, or maid of all work. Most of the servants employed by foreigners in Phnom Penh were Vietnamese. Only a few foreign residents had Cambodian servants – and messy homes. Lanh lived in a room next to the kitchen with her husband, a carpenter, and their small daughter.

Just as the rain ended, three bonzes – young Buddhist monks who lived in a temple down the street – stepped onto the terrace, their cheap cotton umbrellas dripping yellow-dyed rainwater on their bright saffron robes. They held their palms together in front of their chests and moved their hands and bowed their heads in the traditional *namaste*. Julia nodded and smiled and muttered the standard greeting, "*chum reap suo.*"

The monks smiled back and shuffled their feet and looked embarrassed until one stepped forward and said, "Practice English." She invited them in, and they entered, leaving their wet umbrellas on the veranda, and sat on the rattan sofa, looking around with soft brown eyes. The apartment, which Julia's mother would have called "late Salvation Army," with its shabby government-issued sofas and chairs, probably looked luxurious to boys from the Cambodian countryside, she thought.

"You have Pepsi Cola?" asked the lead monk, and she fetched some sodas and a Khmer-English dictionary.

The monks drank their sodas noisily and, between sips, pointed to things in the room and asked, "How you say?"

"Table," Julia would answer, or "floor," and then she would ask how to say it in Cambodian. When she haltingly repeated the Khmer words, they tried not to laugh.

They were very young – their faces smooth with only the barest hint of down on their chins. She asked where they were from, and each shyly said the name of a village. They had come to Phnom Penh to study at the *wat*, or temple, and then would return to their villages. They would not be monks forever. When they finished their sodas, Julia brought another round and the leader said, "America good." She smiled with satisfaction – maybe this was the kind of encounter people meant when they talked about winning the hearts and minds of the people. But, after a time, she began wondering how she could politely get them to leave. They seemed to have settled in. Finally, bells rang from the temple down the street, and, as if on a signal from their leader, they got up and moved toward the door.

Again, they pressed their palms together in the *namaste*, which means both "hello" and "goodbye." Julia tried to imitate the gesture, and the lead bonze went back to the coffee table in front of the sofa and rummaged through the dictionary.

"My divine spark," he said, pointing to his heart. "You divine spark. Our spark bow each other."

She made the gesture again and was rewarded with congratulatory smiles. She kept her palms together as the young monks stepped off the terrace, opening their umbrellas against the resurgent sun.

"*Ils sont partis, mademoiselle?*" asked Lanh, shuffling softly into the room, her black silk trousers and prim white cotton blouse a nun-like contrast to the bright oranges and yellows worn by the monks. A Catholic whose family had fled North Viet Nam when the Communists took over, she seemed to both fear and disdain the Buddhist bonzes. Assured that they had left, she proffered a basket filled with ripe, fragrant mangoes, their bursting flesh covered with skin almost the color of the monks' robes.

"*Les premières mangues, Mademoiselle,*" she said. "Not as good as Viet Nam, but good flavor, I think."

Julia had never tasted a mango. The State Department's Post Report she had read before coming to Cambodia had warned of a mysterious disease called mango fever and of serious skin irritations from the juice. But they looked delicious, so she took the knife Lanh had brought and pierced the surprisingly tough skin, then peeled it away and bit into the soft, sweet fruit. The juice ran down her chin, stinging her skin. But the taste of the succulent flesh, she decided, wiping her chin with a napkin, was worth the momentary pain.

Dinner Chez Harper

From Julia's journal-- This is a serendipitous journal—I never kept one before. But today I took a cyclo-pousse –a sort of bicycle-powered rickshaw – to the Chinese quarter to buy a white shirt for tennis, which I play early in the morning with the young Cambodian coaches, before work and before the heat encases the city in its steamy cocoon... ("La tenue blanche," says the sign on the courts at the Cercle Sportif, "est de rigueur.")... Unlike the rest of Phnom Penh, which is laid out in the French style with wide, tree-lined boulevards and formally planted parks, the quartier chinois is a jumble of narrow streets lined with open-to-the-sidewalk shops that sell everything from teapots to refrigerators to clothing. The merchandise spills out onto the sidewalks, which are crowded with vendors hawking their wares, their loud, sing-song cries competing with music blaring from the shops that sell radios and phonographs. Fortunetellers squat on the pavement, and old men hold cages of songbirds. Dentists set up rudimentary shops on the sidewalks, their primitive tools laid out on less-than-pristine towels.

In the shop where I bought the shirt – really a man's v-neck undershirt – I found a pile of notebooks for sale, the kind with black-and-white marbled covers that I used in grade school. I picked one up and read what was written on the back: "From the schoolchildren of the United States." I raised an eyebrow, but the Chinese shopkeeper just shrugged and grinned, showing a mouthful of gold teeth...I bought one –which is now this journal – but, to tell the truth, I was sort of shocked. We were supposed to be giving these to schoolchildren. When I told this to Bill Harper, the Economic Officer who's taken me under his wing, he laughed and said I had learned more about Cambodia my first week than most senior officers learn in their entire tour...Going there to dinner tonight.

Julia stepped out of the shower and dressed quickly in the darkening bedroom, the ceiling fan giving momentary respite from the lingering heat. The Harpers lived less than half a mile away, but the first time she'd been invited to a dinner party at their house, she had walked and arrived bathed in perspiration. So she stepped outside and nodded to one of the *cyclo* drivers, a wiry man with a dark wrinkled face and shabby, sweat-stained clothes. She climbed into the cab, and he hopped onto the bicycle seat behind the passenger compartment. She directed him through the streets, using the Cambodian words for left, right, and straight, although he probably knew more French than he let on. His broken-veined legs propelled the cab through puddles, which were quickly drying up, down the rue Pasteur, past the shaded stucco villas and apartment houses where the foreigners and upper class Cambodians lived, surrounded by well-kept gardens and lush foliage, and the *paillotes*, straw-roofed houses on stilts where the poorer people lived, whose unkempt front yards were dotted with squat banana trees and where free-ranging chickens rummaged through garbage.

As the sky darkened, the heat which the short, hard mango rains had not banished abated a bit. They wheeled past the Independence Monument, a contemporary paean to the temples of Angkor, whose red sandstone blended with the orange-flagged flame trees, *les flamboyantes*. The *cyclo* made a wide turn and crossed the Boulevard Norodom and headed toward the river. People strolled along the waterfront in what passed for a breeze – the hot brown breath of the Mekong. The strollers ate sugared chunks of pineapple and papaya on sticks that vendors sold from carts along the quay. Families sat by the public fountains, which glowed with colored lights installed for the upcoming visit of the Chinese President, Liu Shao Chi. The illuminated fountains came at a price. Claiming the Cambodians were aiding the Viet Cong, the South Vietnamese had blockaded the Mekong, preventing oil tankers from sailing up the river to Phnom Penh to deliver the fuel needed to produce electricity. Since a festive welcome for the Chinese leader was a priority, Prince Sihanouk rationed electricity in Solomon-like fashion: Each side of the capital had power on alternate nights.

At first, the diplomatic community and other expatriates gave candlelight dinners on the nights they were blacked out, but candles added so much heat and sweat that the dinner- hosting duties shifted to those who had electricity. The Harper's home, a rather grand French colonial villa with a wide veranda, glowed with light.

"*À table, à table* – come sit down," called Helene Harper, an elegant Hong Kong Chinese, wearing a long *cheongsam* of dark green silk that matched her jade earrings. Her sleek black hair was pulled back into a French twist, and her elegant appearance was in sharp contrast to the informality of her husband, who wore a short-sleeved batik shirt that hung loosely over his white cotton slacks.

The guests filed into the high-ceilinged dining room, whose rosewood table was set for eight with Rose Medallion plates and Cambodian silver. The ceiling fan whirred above, its wooden blades stirring the heavy, humid air and blending the odors of the frangipani centerpiece, the musky perfumes worn by the women, and the sweat that gleamed on the faces and bare arms of the guests. As the Vietnamese *boyesse* served the first course of large shrimp in a red, chili-pepper sauce, Bill Harper raised his wine glass in a toast: "Eat, drink and be merry, for tomorrow we'll be dark."

Marie-Claire Marcellini, the petite, peroxide-blonde wife of the Corsica-born director of the École Royale d'Administration, seated on Bill's right, laughed loudly. She wore a black silk dress, whose décolletage drew appreciative glances from Bill. Across the table, Mary, the pregnant American wife of a Cambodian journalist— the dashing, mysterious Bo Samphieu— giggled demurely and seemed to look at her husband for guidance. Bo, who was drinking only water, smiled encouragingly back at her. He was scarecrow thin. His white suit hung loosely on his bony frame, and his hair, which was rather long and straight and blue-black, was constantly being pushed back off his forehead. Though not conventionally handsome, he attracted women like flypaper pins flies. Magda Blair, the bed-hopping Hungarian-born wife of the head of the U.S. aid mission, was said to be crazy about him, and there was always a pretty young "cousin" from the countryside living in his household, a changing *ménage à trois*. His marriage to Mary, the mousy daughter of a now departed American agricultural expert, had surprised everyone. Cynics, including Bill Harper, thought he might want a U.S. visa if things got too dangerous for him, and his marriage ensured that he would get one.

Jake O'Donnell, the handsome young vice-consul, was seated next to Julia. As he talked to Mary, on his left, she studied his profile: dark hair just beginning to recede from a high forehead, beaky nose, generous mouth, liquid brown eyes – the face of a poet, not a staid Foreign Service Officer.

Julia had met Jake in Washington at the Foreign Service Institute, where he was studying Khmer in a small windowless room while she was taking the basic officer training course in a classroom down the hall. They sometimes sat together in the cafeteria and exchanged what little information they had about their future post. When Jake met Ambassador Braithwhite, he was disappointed. He told the ambassador he was studying Khmer and hoped to get out in the countryside and meet ordinary Cambodians, but Braithwhite said in no uncertain terms that, "Prince Sihanouk doesn't want Americans out there riling up the peasants. The embassy will have better uses for your language skills, young man."

Some of the non-American guests had attended the official reception for Liu Shao Chi, whom they described as stern and dour. Americans, of course, played no role in the festivities, and Sihanouk had stepped up the volume of anti-U.S. invective.

"Never mind," said Harper. "That only means we will soon see a warming in U.S.-Cambodian relations as Sihanouk performs another pirouette in his desperate dance of neutrality."

"The word is that, after Liu leaves, the electric power will be restored to normal," ventured Philippe Marcellini, turning to more immediate concerns.

"Perhaps Sihanouk will hold our electricity hostage until South Viet Nam lifts the Mekong blockade," suggested Harper. "Which of course won't work since Washington won't pressure its puppet regime. They don't give a damn about us – still less about Cambodia – certainly not enough to risk ruffling Diem's feathers."

"Bill," said Helene, giving him a warning look, "please pour some more wine for Madame Marcellini."

Harper had consumed most of the first bottle of wine, as well as at least two Scotch-and-waters. His fair-skinned face had reddened, and he was speaking much too freely, Julia realized.

"But there is no evidence Cambodia is aiding the Viet Cong, at least according to your General Edwards, the head of your military mission…" said Marcellini.

"A true diplomat, General Edwards. Quite unlike old striped-pants the Ambassador—." Harper began but was interrupted by his more cautious wife.

"Whose turn is it for the Maugham book?" she asked with a mischievous smile.

A dog-eared copy of Somerset Maugham's *The Painted Veil* was being passed around the expat community, which was titillated by the similarities between Maugham's bed-hopping heroine and the promiscuous Magda Blair.

"Personally, I prefer James Bond," said Harper. "Have you ever noticed how he always starts out with the *left* breast? I wonder if that has political significance…"

"Bill, really," said Helene, while the French couple looked at him quizzically.

Mary eagerly claimed the book, but Bo, seemingly impatient with the frivolous gossip – or perhaps because he had a soft spot for Magda – pointedly asked Harper: "What will your Embassy do about the murder of the American boy by the *cyclo* drivers?"

Shortly before Julia's arrival in Phnom Penh, the body of the 12-year-old son of an American engineer working on the Khmer-American Friendship Highway had been found in the rice fields near Poochentong Airport with multiple stab wounds. The rumor was that the boy repeatedly took pedicabs, and when he had reached his destination, he jumped out and ran without paying the fare, and the *cyclo* drivers, having no legal recourse, got together to deal out rough justice.

"The Ambassador has met with Sihanouk to express our official outrage and to call for a thorough investigation," deadpanned Harper. "And the Prince has graciously agreed. But you should probably talk to our esteemed Press Attaché. His name is Charlie Sherman. You can usually find him on the tennis courts at the Cercle Sportif."

Sherman rarely spoke to the Cambodian press. He saw his job as hobnobbing with foreign correspondents, who rarely showed up in Phnom Penh. At their initial meeting, he had told Julia that she could never be a Press Officer "because, face it, if you stayed out all night drinking with the reporters, they'd get the wrong idea."

"Poor old Braithwhite actually believes there's going to be a real investigation," said Harper scornfully. "The Prince is simply telling him what he wants to hear –he doesn't really expect the Ambassador to believe it. It's a façade. The problem is that the Ambassador doesn't know the rules of the game here – he takes it all literally. He'd do fine in London, or, better still, Ottawa. But he has no grasp of Asia – all off the record, please, Bo."

Harper – and just about everyone else except the Ambassador – knew that nothing would happen. Any investigation of the *cyclo* murder would clearly be a lose/lose proposition for the Prince. If he punished a *cyclo* driver for the murder of a spoiled American boy, the left would turn against him. But if he failed to produce a culprit, he would lose face with the West. And when Sihanouk lost face, he was particularly mercurial and dangerous.

Bo nodded, but didn't smile. In addition to his work as a reporter for the relatively pro-West Phnom-Penh Presse, he was rumored to be an agent of the mysterious Son Ngoc Thanh, leader of an outlawed underground anti-Sihanouk movement known as the Khmers Serei, or Free Khmers.

Bo seemed as if he were about to follow up when a mild commotion sounded at the front door. Sheila Grant, the wife of the Embassy's chief political officer, was speaking loudly in English to the *boyesse*.

"Sheila, come in, come in," said Helene, rising and hurrying to the front door. Sheila, a plump woman in a yellow cotton sundress and white canvas shoes, followed her into the dining room as the entire table fell silent.

"Oh, I'm so sorry, Helene," she said, looking around the table. Sheila may have been pretty at one time but now had the faded, washed-out look of those who do not thrive in the tropics.

"I didn't know you had guests," she said. "I just wondered – do you know what time the commissary board meeting is?"

"No, I'm afraid not," Helene said crisply, ushering Sheila toward the door.

"*Qu'est-ce qu'elle a dit, cette femme?*" asked Marcellini, puzzled, after she had left.

"Oh, she's just a busybody neighbor," replied Harper. "She wanted to see who we were having for dinner. If she spoke any French, she could have asked her maid – they know everything…"

"She's the wife of the Embassy political chief," said Bo, taking a long drag on his cigarette and looking suddenly grim. "Perhaps our conversation will go into a report… Mary, you are looking very tired. Please excuse us, Helene, Bill."

Bo rose quickly, and Mary followed, looking vaguely bewildered. They left the table, and both made the *namaste*. The *boyesse* opened the door, and Mary and Bo disappeared silently into the night.

Although the guests were still finishing the dessert of chilled mango and papaya slices and the obligatory after-dinner drinks had not yet appeared, the interruption and Bo's abrupt departure had broken the spell of the evening, and the other guests started to excuse themselves.

"For Christ's sake," muttered Harper to no one in particular. "I could have reported it if I thought anyone gave a damn about our dinner conversation. Sheila's just prowling around looking for Tom and his girlfriend."

Le tout-Phnom Penh knew that Tom Grant was in love with Elaine Murray, an American teacher of English at the elite Lycée Descartes, but kept a conspiracy of silence about it. Julia wondered whether Sheila suspected. Helene shot Bill a warning look, and he got up to see the departing guests to the door. Julia and Jake were the last to leave.

"I've got my car – let me drive you home, Julia," offered Jake. But when they got into his VW bug, he turned it toward the center of town, away from her apartment.

"Just a newcomer's orientation tour," he explained. "And we need to drink the cognac we would have enjoyed at the Harpers' if that stupid woman hadn't spoiled the mood – and Bo hadn't overreacted. Probably just as well – Harper drank too much, and his bitterness was starting to shine through. He might have said something really nasty about the Ambassador, which would have been all over town by morning."

Bill Harper, Jake explained, still hoped for an ambassadorship. He thought that maybe if he had more experience in the economic sphere – he had always been a political officer – he might have a better shot. He took the post in Phnom Penh to have his economics ticket punched. He was nearing retirement age, and with the State Department's policy of "up or out," this post was his last chance. His fate was in the hands of an ambassador for whom he had scant respect.

Jake parked outside a bar whose neon sign proclaimed it the "Chez Tyna." At the door, a frigid air-conditioned blast from the darkened interior met the sultry night air. Inside, pink lights gave off an eerie glow. The air was thick with cigarette smoke, and American music blared from the jukebox: "Oh, oh, yea, yea, I love you more than I can say." At the bar, men plied the Vietnamese bar girls with expensive drinks that were really just green water. Several of the bar girls waved to Jake, looking Julia up and down in a very unfriendly way.

"These Vietnamese women are my French teachers," Jake said, and Julia suddenly understood how he'd acquired his colorful, colloquial French. "They're just friends – I have a fiancée back home. Her name is Barbara. She's a strict Catholic and doesn't believe in sex before marriage. Do you?"

Julia blushed, and he laughed and patted her hand and said, "Never mind – you don't have to answer."

But, her tongue was loosened by all the wine she had consumed at the Harpers. She said quietly, her words barely audible over the music, "I would have to be in love – really in love – and the man would have to be in love with me."

He raised her chin, so she had to look into his eyes and said, "You stick to that – it's beautiful. But for a man out here …."

He glanced over to a table in the corner of the bar at a woman who seemed a little older than the rest. Small and thin, she reminded Julia of a tiny, brittle-boned bird. She was deep in conversation with a man Julia recognized – a young, crew-cut Marine Guard from the Embassy.

"*Ça va*, Nicole?" called Jake. "How's it going, Chuck?"

The woman smiled at Jake, then turned quickly back to Chuck. The Marine was obviously crazy about her and barely acknowledged Jake's greeting.

"Nicole's a wise woman," he said to Julia. "The Buddhists would say she has an old soul. Chuck fell for her in a big way, and I think she loves him. He's been transferred to Manila. He says he'll send for her. I think he means it – right now."

The cold drink, the icy glares of the bargirls, and the extreme air conditioning made Julia shiver, and she told Jake she wanted to go home.

"I'm not used to starting the workday at 7:30," she said. "And I try to practice tennis before work with the *entraineurs* at the Cercle Sportif."

Despite the fact that the Embassy was air-conditioned, its hours were geared to mesh with those of the Cambodian bureaucracy, which toiled in non-air-conditioned quarters. Work started in the relatively cool morning, and everyone took a long lunchtime *sieste* and then returned to the office in the late afternoon.

"Yes, it takes getting used to," he agreed, but when they got to the car, he insisted on making one more stop and drove to the outskirts of town where Phnom Penh's high-class opium den, or *fumerie* was located. Madame Phuong's was housed in an old, colonial-style mansion set back from the street behind a few scruffy palm trees. As they walked up the steps to the verandah, where a bartender dispensed drinks from a rattan bar, Julia could hear music and laughter from inside, although the long green shutters were closed and the air conditioners were wheezing loudly.

"We'll just sit on the verandah and drink some cognac," Jake said, sensing Julia's discomfort. Madame Phuong's was off limits to Embassy personnel – an edict widely ignored.

Even on the verandah, shielded by shutters from the private smoking lounges, the sweet odor of opium perfumed the night air.

"I didn't want to give you the wrong impression about what I said back in the bar," Jake said earnestly. "It's not that I believe in the double standard. It's just that –oh, hell, you stick to what you said – hold out for real love."

Julia was saved from answering when Joan Pendleton, the Ambassador's secretary, burst noisily out of the house and onto the porch.

An attractive woman in her mid-thirties with hair dyed an improbable shade of red, Joan refused to conform to the Foreign Service Secretary stereotype of the single-woman-with-cat, who sits at home, writes letters, and drinks quietly. Instead, she pursued every available – and not-so-available—man with a desperate flamboyance. Tonight, she had shed her western clothes and donned a sampot, or sarong – apparently customary at Madame Phuong's. Flushed and stumbling with drug or drink or both, she sat down at their table.

"Oh, Jake," she cried, ignoring Julia and looking at him with a mixture of desire and despair.

Jake took her hand.

"Come on, Joanie, I'll take you home," he said, gently. Signaling the waiter to retrieve Joan's clothes, he laid some riels on the table and led Joan to the car.

"Do you mind riding in the back seat?" he asked Julia, apologetically. But she shook her head. She didn't want to be glared at by yet another one of Jake's girlfriends.

"I'll take a *cyclo*," she said firmly.

There were always plenty of *cyclos* lined up in front of Madame Phuong's.

Cercle Sportif

From Julia's journal – Le Cercle Sportif Khmer is a rambling complex with yellow-ochre walls draped in bright magenta bougainvillea. I've started spending my two-hour lunch breaks at the pool there. Most Embassy people think the pool is unhygienic and stay away, so it's mainly the French and other foreigners who use it: diplomats, French fonctionnaires who teach at the École Royale d'Administration – the elite school for rising Cambodian bureaucrats —-teachers from the Lycée Descartes, the handsome Danes who run a company that imports farm machinery, officers from the French military mission. Most upper class Cambodians want their skin to stay light, so they stay out of the sun. (I invited my friend Ket to come to the Cercle with me, but she refused, saying she didn't want to become "foncée comme les paysans" – dark like the peasants.) The Cercle is crowded in the morning, but, around noon, most of the swimmers and sunbathers head out for lunch and a sieste, and you can have the pool more or less to yourself...

"Je veux ma quiche lorraine," said Madame Marcellini plaintively, hurrying her brood through the locker room and bidding Julia *"au revoir."*

Julia put her towel down on a chaise and jumped into the deep end of the long aquamarine pool and began her laps. In the lane next to her, someone passed, doing a strong, smooth breaststroke that made her Australian crawl seem almost frenetic. When she reached the wall on the shallow end, she stopped to rest and watched the other swimmer execute a flawless underwater racing turn and continue swimming. As his body rose above the surface, the water formed droplets on his muscular shoulders and flowed down his tanned back. When he reached the deep end again, he pulled himself out of the pool. Julia hadn't seen him before and wondered who he was. He stopped to chat with Magda Blair, who was sitting under an umbrella, her straw-colored hair tied tightly back from her face with a silk scarf, which accentuated her prominent cheekbones and her slightly slanting gray eyes. Her arms were weighed down with gold jewelry, and her ample girth was barely covered by a flowered bikini that never got wet. (The last time Jake went to Bangkok, the decidedly Junoesque Magda asked him to pick up a bikini she had ordered from her dressmaker there. When the dressmaker brought the bikini to the counter, she held it up and started to giggle uncontrollably. She had probably never seen a bikini quite that wide. Jake confessed that he had laughed, too.)

After a few minutes, Magda called out in her raspy Hungarian-accented voice, "Julia, darling, come here. I want to introduce Monsieur Hourani, the new Moroccan chargé d'affaires."

Julia nodded and waved but resumed swimming.

Did Magda really think she would jump out of the pool to be presented as some sort of specimen? she thought indignantly. He was awfully attractive though, she decided, sneaking a glance at his sleek body, glistening with water. He was of medium height, with wavy brown hair, a hawk-like nose and slightly hooded blue eyes – the legacy of a French grandmother, she learned later.

But why wasn't Magda-the-man-eater keeping him to herself? Harper described her as a woman who couldn't remember whose bed she had left her shoes under, and she was said to prefer younger men.

By the time she finished her laps, the man was gone, and she felt oddly disappointed. After that initial encounter – really an encounter manqué – she sometimes saw him at parties and functions, but, though they nodded and smiled to each other, they never spoke until a reception celebrating Hungary's National Day.

The garden of the Hungarian ambassador's residence was hung with colored lights and packed with overdressed people wilting in the heat. Julia was chatting with a man from the Indonesian Embassy, who turned suddenly to greet a tall Chinese man in a high-necked uniform – the Chinese ambassador. The ambassador bowed slightly to Julia and started to proffer his hand, and then an aide whispered something in his ear, and he dropped his hand and turned his back. The aide must have told him she was American, and of course, the two countries didn't speak.

There was a buzz in the room, and people stared and moved away from Julia as if she had committed a social gaffe. She was embarrassed and at a loss for what to do when she felt a firm hand under her elbow. She turned and looked into the clear blue eyes of the man from the swimming pool, Monsieur Hourani.

"Don't let it trouble you, *mademoiselle*," he said, smiling and keeping hold of her arm. "It's only politics. Come, let's go to the buffet."

He steered her out of the garden and up into the house, which was darker and cooler. He filled a plate with some hors d'oeuvres and led her to a corner of the living room. They sat on the sofa, and Julia began to relax and see the humor in the situation.

"Since we have been introduced, after a fashion, by the estimable Madame Blair, perhaps you would consent to have dinner with me tonight?" he said. "I think you'd like to leave this party, and I would, too. And maybe a film afterward. Isn't that what you'd be doing on a Friday evening in the States?"

Julia thought fleetingly of her Friday night dates in college – hamburgers in a bar and a movie in the local theater—and thought how different this would be, a world away. But she nodded yes, and they walked out the front door without even making their farewells. Hourani's driver waited across the street, in a black Mercedes with bright red Moroccan flags on both sides of the front windshield. Hourani spoke to him briefly in Arabic and handed him some money. The driver got out and opened the passenger door for Julia, and Hourani got behind the wheel.

"Where shall we go?" he asked. "Have you been to the Café de Paris? The food is excellent."

"Yes," she replied. "I mean, no, I haven't been there, but that would be… lovely."

"Good," he said. "*Allons-y.*"

He started the car, and Julia sank back into the soft leather seat and kept stealing glances at him as he drove down the wide Boulevard Norodom. He wore a dark blue suit, but she could see the outline of his muscular shoulders beneath the expensive-looking material and remembered how he had looked at the pool. At the restaurant, the maître d' greeted him by name and seated them by a window looking out on the leafy garden, lit by small candles. The Café de Paris sat on the edge of the posh neighborhood where most of the French residents of Phnom Penh lived. French residents and European diplomats made up most of its clientele, and Cambodians – unless they were government officials – usually received a chilly reception.

Julia ordered coquilles Saint-Jacques, and Hourani nodded approvingly and ordered another seafood dish and a bottle of white wine.

"Where did you learn your excellent French?" he asked, as the waiter silently opened the chilled bottle and poured just the right amount into each glass.

"I studied in Paris – my junior year," she explained, "but I know I have a terrible accent, in spite of all those phonetics classes."

"You have a charming accent," he protested. "Were you at Reid Hall? I was at *Sciences Po'*, but several years before you, I imagine. I am an old man – I will soon turn thirty. You must come to my birthday celebration." His eyes lingered on hers. "So, already we have much in common. We both studied in Paris, and we both like to swim."

"And you – where did you learn your excellent English?" she asked.

"My first post was Washington," he answered. "That's how I know about the Friday night dinner and a movie. But tell me more about you. Where exactly in the States do you come from?"

"Philadelphia," she answered. "Or just outside. There's really not much to tell. I went to college in Massachusetts, spent a year in Paris, took the Foreign Service exam, and here I am."

"And you are obviously highly intelligent," he said. "I know it's a difficult exam, and I suspect they select very few women."

It was true there were only five other women in her Foreign Service class, and they had been told they would have to resign if they married. ("That's why we don't hire many women," the rather patronizing personnel officer had said. "They quit – they have to when they get married – and we don't recoup the training cost.")

"Tell me more about you," she said, and he told her his father was a civil servant in Rabat, and his mother a teacher in the French *lycée* there. His older brother was a doctor.

"We would have liked a sister," he added, his eyes twinkling in a way that made her heart flutter though she felt far from sisterly toward him.

The restaurant, which they had had more or less to themselves until now, began to fill. Several people greeted Hourani, nodding to Julia in a friendly way that made her feel she had overcome the embarrassment at the Hungarian Embassy. The women were elegantly dressed in silks and jewels, and Julia regretted that she had worn her plain black linen shift, already faded and looking worn from Lanh's frequent laundering. How did these women do it? she wondered. Dry cleaning was non-existent in Phnom Penh, and makeup tended to melt in the heat.

The Marcellinis entered with a large, noisy party.

"*Tiens!*" said Madame Marcellini, rushing to their table. Hourani rose to greet her, and she took his face in her hands and kissed him on both cheeks. "*Vous vous connaissez? Mais, c'est parfait,*" she added, grinning at Julia.

The news of their "date" – or whatever the French called it – would quickly be common knowledge. Marie-Claire

Marcellini was a notorious gossip. Not that Julia really minded. She smiled to herself.

"Now, what about the film?" said Hourani, interrupting her reverie. "There's a Jerry Lewis film at the Ciné Luxe. He makes you laugh, and I think that's what you need after that silly snub by the Chinese ambassador."

Julia would never have gone to a Jerry Lewis movie by choice, but she readily agreed.

I'd probably go anywhere with him, she thought as they entered the dark, makeshift theatre – really a converted garage.

When they were seated, he took a pair of his glasses out of his pocket and put them on, and she loved the way he looked in them, vulnerable somehow. She felt tender toward him, and when he reached for her hand, she returned the pressure.

I guess I'm falling in love, she decided as she watched him laugh at Lewis' antics, and she laughed herself until the tears streamed down her cheeks. On the drive home, they laughed some more, but as they neared her apartment, she began to get nervous.

Should I ask him in? she wondered, wanting to but afraid.

He parked the car and reached across her to open the car door. Their eyes locked for a moment and he smiled. Then they both got out of the car, and he walked her to the door and bent down and kissed her hand.

"Good night," he said. "Sleep well."

Chamcar Mon

From Julia's journal—I hardly slept at all last night, wondering if we'd see each other again, wondering what I'll do if we do see other again... The men – boys, really – I had known in college always tried to get you into bed, but really expected you to fight them off. The European men I knew in Paris weren't like that. If you wouldn't go to bed with them, they quickly lost interest. I don't want Charles Hourani to go away, but it's true what I told Jake: I want to wait until I'm sure it's real love —on both sides.

"*Bonsoir, Mademoiselle,*" said Lanh as Julia stepped out of a *cyclo* the next evening after work. Lanh didn't usually come to the curb to greet her, so Julia wondered if anything was wrong.

"You have letter," said the Vietnamese woman. "Car, driver bring."

Julia took the note, on Moroccan Embassy stationery, her hands trembling a bit as she opened it.

"*Chère mademoiselle*," it read. "Will you do me the honor of attending Prince Sihanouk's volleyball tournament this evening at Chamcar Mon? I must play on the *corps diplomatique* team, and, afterwards, we can have dinner together."

The Prince hosted weekly volleyball matches at his residence on the outskirts of Phnom Penh. Named for the silkworm fields that surrounded it, Chamcar Mon was about as far from the Royal Palace and his dotty mother as he could get and still be in the capital.

Julia quickly showered and changed and hailed a *cyclo*, directing the driver down the surprisingly rough road to Chamcar Mon. Unlike the rest of Phnom Penh, which was manicured and lush, the area had a raw newness about it with a lot of villas under construction, their yards barren of plantings.

The security guard at Chamcar Mon waved her through. The games were in full swing, and she took a seat on the bleachers. Princess Monique's team of palace women had, predictably, just defeated a team called simply "*femmes françaises*," and the Prince was cheering loudly from the sidelines. The grounds were lit, but the sky overhead was dark and heavy with the monsoon rains that would, very soon, inundate the land. A light rain was falling and between matches, Prince Sihanouk, smiling graciously, distributed bright yellow cotton umbrellas – the kind the Buddhist bonzes carry – to the spectators. Later, as the Prince's team battled it out with the U.S. military mission, Julia noticed one of General Edward's aides furiously taking notes on a clipboard.

"Why do you take it so seriously?" she chided the young officer, whom she knew slightly. "It's only a game."

"Yes," he replied without looking up from his notes. "But it's the most important game in Cambodia."

When Hourani's match was finished, he came up and took her hand and led her away from the bleachers.

"The Americans are the only ones that try to beat the Prince's team," he whispered. "Why? It's stupid, self-defeating. This is diplomacy – not volleyball."

"We Americans take our games seriously," she laughed. He shrugged, and they set off to explore the grounds.

Amazingly, given Sihanouk's well-known paranoia, there seemed to be little security other than the guard at the gate – no one seemed to care that they were wandering about. Behind the sprawling, one-story Mediterranean-style villa surrounded by lush plumeria and towering mango trees, they stumbled upon the Prince's heart-shaped swimming pool, built when he married Monique, a beautiful half-Italian, half-Laotian woman.

"Care for a swim?" he joked, but then it started to rain a little harder, and he pulled her into the pool house and took her in his arms. She could smell his sweat from the volleyball game mixed with the heady scent of rain-drenched plumeria and jasmine blossoms in the sultry air, and her ears filled with an exquisite pressure, and her throat, too, so that she could barely breathe.

"I am too old for cement floors," he said, and he grabbed her hand and they ran through the now pelting rain to his car and drove to his bungalow, a pink-stucco cottage in a grove of poinciana trees behind the Hotel Royale. Once inside the starkly impersonal interior, Julia felt shy with him, a little afraid. He seemed to understand and put a record on the stereo, and as they danced, he sang the words in her ear:

"Te quiero mucho, mucho, mucho..."

In Spanish, the words for "love" and "want" seemed to be interchangeable, and as he put his tongue into her ear and pulled her body against his, the difference no longer mattered to Julia either. He led her into the bedroom, and they removed each other's clothes. Julia wanted him terribly, but all she could feel was the pain, like a hammer pounding through her flesh. Then, suddenly, the barrier was gone, and he filled her for a tantalizing moment, then withdrew, spilling his semen on the bloodied sheets. "Next time, I will have a condom," he whispered, kissing her on the forehead, "and you will feel much pleasure and no more pain."

He took her in his arms and held her, stroking her long hair. She reached for his hand and kissed it.

"I should go," she said finally, and he started to dress to drive her home, but she said no, that she would take a *cyclo*.

They argued about that a little, but finally he acquiesced. Julia couldn't explain, but she wanted to be alone, to savor the important thing that had just happened. He kissed her goodbye at the door, and she lingered in his arms, kissing his neck, then finally broke away. As she left the bungalow area, still in a daze, she ran headlong into Jake, who was coming out of the bar.

"Whoa," he said, "What are you doing here? If I didn't know you better…"

"But you don't know me better," she replied, avoiding his gaze.

She tried to brush past him, but he put a hand on her arm and looked at her with a mixture of concern and disapproval.

"I hope you're not getting involved with Charles Hourani," he said, looking in the direction of Hourani's bungalow. "He's the playboy of the western world. And what happened to real love? I'm disappointed in you Julia."

Again, she tried to break free, but he tightened his grasp and gave her arm a shake.

"You're not at Mount Holyoke anymore. These people don't play by the same rules," he said, but he let go of her arm and she hurried through the now empty hotel lobby to the *cyclo* stand.

It was raining harder now, and the *cyclo* driver had put a plastic tarp around the passenger cab. The *cyclo* swished through the wet streets, silent except for the splashing sounds the wheels made in the deep puddles. Julia felt enclosed in her own private world, where Jake's warning could not penetrate and spoil her elated mood.

Concours d'Élégance

From Julia's journal –I had always thought that when I finally went to bed with someone it would be the real thing, the one and only thing, and, for me, I think it is. My body feels a frisson of excitement each time I see him, but it isn't only that. I love talking with him, learning about him, seeing him as a little boy. But maybe for him, I'm just someone new to go to bed with. Perhaps I am, as Jake implied, just a name in an overflowing black book...

Hourani's Mercedes hummed long, dodging the ubiquitous potholes on the Khmer-American Friendship Highway, which led from Phnom Penh to the port of Sihanoukville and the beaches on the Gulf of Siam. Water buffalo grazed beside the road, against a backdrop of emerald green rice fields. Small villages appeared at intervals, the only variation on the relentlessly flat landscape.

"Do you want a coffee?" he asked Julia as they approached Kompong Speu.

She nodded, and he pulled into the gas station/café at the crossroads, which sold the coffee sweetened with condensed milk that Cambodians love. The flies loved it too, and they had to run from the café to the car to escape the swarm. They were en route to Kep, which Cambodians touted as "the St. Tropez of Southeast Asia," for the *Concours d'Élégance*, an event patterned after similar contests on the Côte d'Azur: Attractive, well-dressed women stepped out of shiny luxury cars, and both were admired by the applauding crowd.

Julia's friend Elaine Murray, a young American who taught English at the elite high school, the Lycée Descartes, would be in a Chevy Impala at the request of the one local automobile dealer who sold American cars – the first time in anyone's memory an American woman had participated. ("Of course, she won't win," Harper had predicted. "It would be political suicide for the judges if they picked an American car and an American woman.")

Hourani had to attend, because Sihanouk would award the prizes and it was *de rigueur* for the diplomatic corps to be there. Julia was happy to go because she loved the beach and because she wanted to be with him. He had booked separate rooms at the Auberge de Kep, set among luxe villas on the long palm-shaded corniche above the sea. After they checked in and changed, they met in the lobby to go to the beach.

"When I was at Sciences Po'," he said, "we rented scooters during a break and rode down to St. Tropez. It took two days, and when we finally got there, we had no money left. We slept on the beach. It looked something like this. He surveyed the yellow-sand beach fringed with a shaded walkway, nodding and waving to a few acquaintances, including Ang Khem, a Cambodian army officer who was with Denise Foletti, the lovely half-Vietnamese daughter of the Italian Fiat dealer in Phnom Penh. Denise wore a wide-brimmed white hat over her shiny black hair. Large sunglasses hid her vaguely almond-shaped eyes, and a yellow bikini set off her honey-colored skin.

She looks even younger than I am, thought Julia.

A beach attendant set up chairs for them, but Julia was hot and went right into the water and swam out fifty feet or so in the tepid, waveless sea, then floated on her back. The sky was overcast, heavy with the unfulfilled promise of rain.

Julia swam slowly back to the beach, and Hourani, restless, wanted to leave.

"I think we've had enough sun," he said. He waved to Ang Khem and nodded to Denise, and they went back to his room and made love under the sluggishly churning ceiling fan, which failed to disperse the thick, humid air.

He's just going through the motions, Julia thought fearfully. He seems bored, enervated, but maybe it's just the heat.

"Let's go to that place on the river," he proposed, quickly putting on his clothes. They drove into the hills and parked the car and walked down a path to a spot on the Tuk Chhu River, where the water formed cool pools and there were rocks to sit on. There were usually a lot of country people there in their sarong-like *sampots*, cooling off, but it was late, and they had it to themselves. They bought a *sampot* from a vendor who stood by the road, undressed and wrapped their naked bodies together in the garment and let the cool water wash away the languor and odor of sex.

It was almost dark when they got back to the hotel. People were gathering on the terrace for aperitifs, and there was a buzz of anticipation about tomorrow's *Concours*. Elaine Murray sat alone at a table, nursing a glass of white wine. She had dark, almost blue-black hair, a turned-up nose, bright, intelligent green eyes and pale skin that tended to freckle in the sun, making her look younger than her 27 years. Though not a classic beauty, Elaine had the fresh-faced good looks people associated with the ideal American girl – probably why the car dealer had enlisted her to drive a Chevy Impala. She didn't care. It was a wonderful excuse to spend a weekend with Tom Grant, her married lover. 'Married lover.' She repeated the phrase silently – it was something she never thought she'd say or do, having grown up in a strict Irish Catholic family on Chicago's south side. Even worse, she knew in her heart it would end badly – then he'd never leave his wife. But she put that out of her mind and thought only of the night – the first full night they would spend together.

As the Embassy political chief, Tom was ostensibly coming to report on Sihanouk's conduct at the event – how he behaved toward the American car, for example, would be duly reported to Washington, though it was doubtful anyone there would really care. Normally, they had only late afternoons, when Tom would come to her apartment on the Quai Sisowath and they would make love and then drink aperitifs on her balcony and watch the darkness fall and the lights come on in the boats on the river, a signal that he had to go home to Sheila.

They had met when she first came to Phnom Penh the year before and he gave her a political briefing – the unclassified version since she wasn't part of the Embassy staff but a teacher under the Fulbright program. Because she was an attractive single woman who spoke fluent French, she was often invited to diplomatic functions, so they saw each other fairly often. One rainy afternoon during the last monsoon season, he walked into an air-conditioned trailer in the Ancien Marché, which was Elaine's favorite bookstore. Its shelves were lined with yellowing French *livres de poche*, and the proprietor played scratched records of classical music on an old record player. Elaine's straw market basket was already filled with books, and Tom offered to help her carry it home.

Someone came up the steps of the hotel, but it wasn't Tom. She waved to her friend Julia and her Moroccan boyfriend, whom Elaine didn't quite trust. Julia hurried through to her room, but Hourani lingered on the terrace and sat down at a table with Denise Foletti and Ang Khem. Then Tom came up the steps, carrying a suitcase, and Elaine thought only of him. As they had agreed, they didn't greet each other there. Instead, Elaine went upstairs to her room to wait.

When Julia had changed for dinner, she knocked at Hourani's door and found him sitting on the bed reading travel brochures.

"I want to go to the Great Barrier Reef," he announced casually, looking up briefly from the colorful booklet.

He also had material on Tahiti and Fiji and Bali.

Julia gave him a puzzled look, and he explained, rather impatiently, "You remember, I told you I've been planning a trip around the world."

She was stunned. He had mentioned it once, but she had assumed it was a someday thing, and that since they were in love, he would drop the idea.

"Probably around the first of the year – after our new Ambassador arrives," he said. "I have some leave coming."

"Oh," she said, trying to smile noncommittally.

They went down to dinner, but Julia had lost her appetite and picked at her *fruits de mer* in a numb daze –she felt like she had been kicked in the stomach. She had thought – hoped – that they would be making plans together, but his plan clearly didn't include her. *What about me?* she wanted to ask. *What about us?*

"Look, *chérie*, the trip is six months away," he said, putting his hand over hers. "And I will not disappear off the edge of the earth."

She didn't look convinced, and he began to get annoyed.

"You American women are so possessive," he said, practically glaring at her, then adding, a little more gently, "You are young. You will learn that life is not like one of those American films with that perky blonde actress – what's her name? Doris Day. Real life is so much more interesting."

When the music started, he asked her to dance. She longed for a slow dance, so she could nestle in his arms, but it was something with a Latin beat. He had been posted in Rio and knew all the Latin American dances. Julia was, at best, a mediocre dancer, but she managed to keep up and follow his lead through the complex movements.

Soon, there were only two couples left on the floor. Denise Foletti was dancing almost as in a trance with Ang Khem. Khem was as awkward and stiff as Julia, and Julia suddenly felt that she and Ang Khem weren't there at all, that their partners, though they never touched, were somehow dancing with each other. When the music stopped, the people at the tables applauded enthusiastically. Hourani bowed to Denise, who smiled at him, a smile that seemed to light up the restaurant. He and Julia went to his room and slept, without making love.

The next day, the rains held off until just after the *Concours*. Elaine wore a flowered sundress and looked lovely as she stepped out of the white Impala convertible. Everyone cheered, and Julia knew that Tom was in the crowd and that it was his applause that mattered to Elaine.

Denise, in a clingy red dress and a Fiat *Floride*, was declared the winner, and Prince Sihanouk hung a gold medal around her slender neck.

Vernissage

From Julia's journal –Salt. Sweat. Tears. In his room, under the sluggish ceiling fan, our bodies glistened with sweat, which tasted salty when I licked him. Funny that sweat tastes like tears...

"If you see any insects, brush them out of the way – then spray," Saria, the Cambodian librarian at the American Library, instructed the workmen, bowing to Buddhist reluctance to take any life but relentlessly getting the building ready for the *vernissage*, the opening of an art exhibit of paintings that would appear on the Embassy-produced calendar. The artists were the best students and teachers at the École Royale des Beaux Arts, but the paintings were, in truth, quite pedestrian—lots of contented water buffalo in rice paddies. Julia was charged with choosing appropriate quotations from Sihanouk for each month's painting, but all she could find were earthy exhortations about growing two crops of rice per year. (This was a constant theme of his, but the peasants seemed to shrug as if to say, "Why bother? We have enough to eat.")

Hors d'oeuvres were waiting under mesh coverings that kept out insects. Waiters passed among the guests with trays of glasses filled with highballs and gin-tonics and orange juice, the ice cubes quickly melting. Others carried trays of cigarettes and lighted candles. Members of the Embassy staff, ordered to arrive early to host the event, were already grabbing drinks off the trays.

"The Ambassador has engaged the winning artist to paint the numbers on his license plate. Isn't that true, Joan?" Harper asked, grabbing the Ambassador's secretary by the arm. In Cambodia, the government assigned license plate numbers but left it to the car owner to supply the actual plate.

"Sure, Bill, if you say so," she replied, and looked around distractedly, scanning the room, probably for Jake, who had not yet shown up. A Vassar dropout, Joan had a brassy beauty that went with her deep, husky voice, which heavy drinking had deepened.

Julia felt some empathy with Joan as she scanned the room for Hourani, who had promised to come and take her to dinner afterward. An Italian restaurant had opened in

Phnom Penh – a major event in a place where little happened – and the chef, a Vietnamese who had apprenticed at a restaurant in Venice, had won rave reviews.

The library was beginning to fill and to heat up, and faces glistened with sweat. Sheila Grant was chatting with Ambassador Braithwhite's wife, while her husband, Tom, was on the other side of the room pretending to study one of the paintings, Elaine at his side. Her long dark hair was tied back in its habitual ponytail, and she was short enough that she could look up at Tom, who wasn't very tall. When he looked at Elaine, his broad, rather homely face lit up and became almost handsome, Julia thought. The power of love.

She spotted one of her contacts from the Cambodian Ministry of Information and crossed the room to greet him.

"*Bonsoir, mademoiselle,*" he said with a broad smile, praising the exhibit and thanking her for the Embassy's plan to produce the calendar.

"I hope the calendar will pass your censors with no problem, *monsieur,*" Julia responded, also smiling.

The current issue of the Embassy magazine was being held up by the Ministry censors because it showed a photograph of a school with thatch walls.

"Cambodia is a modern country. Our schools do not have thatch walls," the Minister had told the Ambassador, who merely nodded and instructed the Public Affairs Officer to fix the problem. The Minister wasn't worried about what the Cambodian readers of the magazine might think. They, of course, knew that many Cambodian schools had thatch walls. Although the magazine was published in Khmer and distributed exclusively in Cambodia, the official apparently feared it might fall into foreign hands, causing his country to lose face with the world. The story was about Americans who taught in Cambodia under the Fulbright program, and the censorship problem had already been solved. The Cambodian production staff brought in some of their friends, and in one day, cut the offending picture out of all 5,000 copies of the magazine.

The ministry official looked embarrassed – but more for Julia than for himself. She had broken a cardinal rule of Cambodian etiquette: Never confront anyone, and certainly not at a social event.

"None of it matters anyway, kid," said Harper, who had overheard the conversation. He grabbed a Scotch – clearly not his first – from a passing waiter.

"All the magazines, all the art exhibits in the world, all the perfumes of Arabia... None of it matters a damn," he said, downing the Scotch. "Dulles is dead, but neutralism is suspect – you're either with or against us. And Sihanouk, whose word is law here, is committed to neutrality. It's the only way he thinks he can survive. And our closest allies here – South Viet Nam and Thailand – are his historical enemies. Are we really naïve enough to believe that the fact that an American finds some goddamned antelope in the mountains means anything at all?"

A zoologist from the National Academy of Sciences had recently found a *ko prey* in the mountains near Ratanakiri. A rare species of gazelle and Cambodia's national animal, the *ko prey* had long been considered extinct. The Embassy was trying to wring some goodwill out of this, but few Cambodians seemed interested.

"Anyway, I'm not sure any of these people matter either," he continued, making a sweeping gesture around the room with the arm that didn't have a drink in it. "Look outside at the man sweeping the street, or the guy pedaling the *cyclo*. Do we have any inkling of what they're thinking? Maybe someday, they'll tell us, and I'll bet it won't be pretty... Maybe we got just a hint of that in the murder of the American boy."

His voice had been growing louder and louder, and people were beginning to stare. Fortunately, the watchful

Helene came up and took his arm, leading him tactfully away. Julia took a *tonique nature* – plain tonic, the only way she could survive cocktail parties in the heat – and went to join Ang Khem, who was conversing in French with Magda. She was perspiring profusely in a too-tight, sequined dress and eyeing Khem with a hungry look. Surely, he was too short to be one of her lovers, Julia thought. But a walleye made Khem rather dashing, and Magda was reputed to have eclectic tastes.

"Felicitations, mon capitaine," Julia greeted him, earning a glare from Magda.

The young officer laughed.

Prince Sihanouk had recently organized a *Soirée Théâtrale* to benefit one of his mother's pet causes, the restoration of the Silver Pagoda next to the Palace. The one-act plays were directed by the Prince, who played most of the starring roles opposite his wife. Ang Khem had played a supporting role, as the Prince's valet in a piece entitled, *The Ideal Husband.* Although Khem was only a lieutenant, Sihanouk had addressed him as *"mon capitaine"* during rehearsals, and the program listed him as Capitaine Ang Khem. The army had no choice but to give him a field promotion.

"I am giving a party to celebrate my promotion, *mademoiselle*," he said. "Will you do me the honor of attending?"

She promised to come, then excused herself to find Hourani, who was surrounded by several members of Phnom Penh's *jeunesse dorée* – the sons and daughters of Cambodian officials and French and other foreign residents, many of whom did little except drive around town in fast sports cars. Julia had met many of them through her friend Ket, who wasn't really part of their set but knew them from her days at the Lycée Descartes.

"Let's go and eat *jao-tse*," someone suggested, and the rest took up the idea enthusiastically. Hourani looked at Julia as if to say, "what can I do?" and she knew the Italian restaurant would have to wait for another evening. Julia liked *jao-tse*, and she liked going to the bicycle shop on the Boulevard Monivong where, in the evening, the storeowner's wife steamed the pork-filled Chinese dumplings in a big vat and served them on picnic tables in the side yard. But she felt uncomfortable going there with this noisy, overdressed crowd. Besides, she had counted on being alone with Hourani. Things had been awkward between them since the weekend in Kep, and she was still trying to get some assurance that his round-the-world trip wouldn't mean the end of their relationship.

"Don't pout, *chérie*," he whispered as she climbed into the front seat of his Mercedes next to him. Denise Foletti, in a low-cut cerise dress, sat in the backseat on the lap of a young Cambodian army lieutenant who had a French wife but never brought her to parties.

Hourani was wearing a silk shirt, and Julia's arm brushed against it. She longed to rub her face against the material, and then unbutton it and press her lips against his chest.

Instead, she congratulated Denise on her win at the Concours d'Élégance and received a cool, silent smile in return.

They parked near the shop, and the night air was heavy and hot and smelled of river mud. It was very dark, and there were no stars, but the inside of the bicycle shop was illumined with candles. At the back of the shop, in front of a wall hung with bicycle wheels, was an improvised altar covered with oranges, bottles of Chinese wine, and other offerings. Above the altar hung a photograph of the shopowner, and incense burners sent their sweet fumes into the still air. People, all dressed in white, sat on folding chairs around a garishly painted coffin, eating sweet cakes and drinking tea. The owner's wife shed her apron and was lighting a joss stick and bowing before the makeshift altar. She turned and saw the group and smiled falteringly, then gestured to them to come in.

They hung back. It was too late to leave unnoticed. Hourani stepped forward, depositing a hundred riel note in the basket by the altar and then turning and leading the group toward the car. There would be no *jao-tse* there tonight, or probably ever again. They had unwittingly stepped into the funeral of the shopowner.

Denise clutched Hourani's arm, as if afraid.

"*Il est mort, le chinois*," she breathed. "The Chinese is dead."

She lifted her face to Hourani, her lower lip trembling and her brown eyes liquid with tears. He touched her arm gently, and when Julia saw the tender look that passed between them, she knew at once she had lost him. When he took her home, Julia tried to talk, but he silenced her with a perfunctory kiss. He said good night, and they both knew he meant goodbye.

Danses Macabres

From Julia's journal –I went to Ang Khem's party, hoping Hourani would be there alone and that he would tell me that he loved me and that the flirtation with Denise had been a terrible mistake, but, of course, it didn't happen that way. My friend Ket was there and told me that Hourani had just left – with Denise. I pretended not to care and drank too much. Ang Khem had arranged for a photographer, and the next day, I went around to the photo shop and bought all the photos of me I could find, not because I wanted them but because I didn't want anyone to see pictures of me obviously a bit drunk. I tried not to look at the pictures of Hourani and Denise. On the way home from the shop, I walked past the Palace stables when the royal elephants – they are called white but are actually pinky-gray albinos – were being washed. The Buddhists say that elephants are the only animals that remember their former lives, and spend long hours contemplating the past.

As she climbed the outside steps to the Chan Chaya pavilion on the grounds of the Royal Palace, Julia could hear the xylophones and gongs and oboes and cymbals that made up the Palace orchestra. When she first heard Khmer music, the flat atonal sounds seemed almost grating, like shrieks, but she soon came to appreciate the way there were no crescendos, the way it simply went on and on until it became hypnotic, without any real high or low points. Like the Buddhist concept of life, the music was a continuum.

The musicians were seated cross-legged on the marble floor of the open-walled pavilion set on the Palace grounds amid gardens of blood-red hibiscus and ponds filled with pink and yellow lotus blossoms. Huge teak pillars held up the steep-pitched roof, whose eaves swept skyward, tipped with wing-like gilt furbelows called "tongues of fire." The roof amplified the sound of the rain, which fell in sheets, drenching the gardens and enclosing the pavilion in a curtain of water. Petite dancers, members of the Royal Cambodian Ballet, were going through their slow, stylized movements, while much larger American dancers – members of the New York modern dance troupe the Embassy was hosting – watched admiringly from the sidelines.

"In Cambodian ballet, the dancers are *apsaras*, handmaidens in a celestial garden. In the dance, they give their bodies back to the gods who created them," an interpreter from the Ministry of Information explained.

"It's so nuanced, so formal," gushed Rod Lupino, the leader of the American troupe. "I hadn't realized that it's really very sexual."

The interpreter blushed, and some of the dancers giggled, although the remark probably wasn't translated literally. Princess Bopha Devi, Sihanouk's daughter and the prima ballerina, offered to teach the American dancers some of the basic movements—Julia's cue to send the Embassy photographer into action. He snapped away as the other Cambodian dancers, following Bopha Devi's lead, took the Americans and physically moved their hands in the formal movements of the ballet. Although they had the slender, well-muscled bodies of dancers, the Americans all looked clunky and awkward beside their Cambodian counterparts. The pictures would be used in the Embassy magazine to show the bond between the Cambodian and American dancers – the universality of art or something like that – but Julia suspected the local readers would only titter at the contrast between the clumsy foreigners and the graceful Cambodians.

Bopha Devi whispered to the interpreter, who then asked if the Americans would show some of their movements, which, of course, was the plan all along. Rod and the lead female dancer, took the floor in a slow sensual *pas de deux* that ended when he lifted her into the air. The Cambodians applauded, many whispering among themselves, probably about Rod's erection, painfully visible through his flesh-colored tights. Later, however, Rod charmed the Cambodian dancers by clasping his hands together in a *namaste*, which Julia had taught him, to say goodbye.

"We are thrilled at the prospect of seeing Angkor Wat," he told them, "and the privilege of dancing there."

Transporting the dance troupe and the required equipment to Angkor would be logistical nightmare, but Rod had insisted on performing there.

"I'm only coming to Cambodia because my wife wants to see Angkor Wat," he'd said.

The Embassy had reluctantly agreed.

"Does that idiot in tights realize it's the rainy season?" asked Harper.

Loud clouds hung over Poochentong Airport as the dancers and a large contingent from the Embassy boarded a Royal Air Cambodge plane for the short flight to Siem Reap the next day. A truck, loaded with lights and sound equipment had left the day before, despite warnings that rains had made parts of the road impassable. The plan – negotiated by Rod – was for the dancers to have a full day to rest and tour the temples. The performance would take place the day after that, giving the crew time to set up the stage, on the wide terrace in front of Angkor Wat.

"It's so vast," exclaimed Rod, as a guide led the group around the complex. They had given the dancers the afternoon to rest at the aging Grand Hotel, waiting for the temperature to go down a little. But it was still very hot, and the heavy, humid air seemed to encroach on the temple like the surrounding jungle.

"Angkor Wat is only one of many temples in the complex – albeit perhaps the most important one," explained the guide. "We are still making discoveries. We are not sure how many more wonders the jungle holds. In the 12th century, Angkor Thom – or Angkor city – had a population of about 750,000 – more people than live in Phnom Penh today. Most were workers needed to carry the rocks that had been ferried up the river to build the temples."

"Thank God for slave labor," quipped Harper *sotto voce* to Julia.

"I think we need to cut it short," she said. "We'll never be able to see everything."

She went ahead to have a word with the guide, who readily agreed. They would stick to the outer terraces of Angkor Wat, admiring the elaborate bas reliefs, briefly explore Angkor Thom and, then, at Julia's request, peek at her favorite temple, the jewel-like, jungle-enclosed Ta Prohm.

"Just be sure we don't miss the phallic symbol. Rod will love that," said Harper, referring to the *linga-raj*, the snake-like penis that personified Shiva or creative energy.

"On the left side of the Giant's Causeway guarding the entrance of Angkor Thom, you see 54 gods," the guide was intoning. "On the right are 54 devils."

"Ah, the key to Sihanouk's foreign policy," Harper whispered, and Julia tried not to laugh. "And now we'll admire the four identical royal heads facing four different directions – at least Sihanouk only has two faces."

"There's such a sweet smell here," Rod's wife said. Julia didn't have the heart to tell her the odor was incense mixed with the dung of the bats that slept in the temple by day, flying out noisily at dusk.

It was a fair distance to Ta Prohm. The dancers' energy seemed to be flagging, and Julia was having second thoughts. Was she only dragging them here because she and Hourani had made love in its vine-tangled courtyard?

The sky was darkening with either nightfall or rain or both as they approached. The many trees that rose high above the towers dappled what light was left, casting greenish shadows over the crumbling temple walls. Chunks of stone dislodged by gnarled tree roots lay scattered on the narrow pathway.

Julia momentarily lost herself in the temple's spell and in her memory of Hourani but was quickly brought to reality by a shrill scream.

"My ankle – I think it's broken," Rod's wife writhed in agony. The heel of her sandal was caught in a tangle of banyan roots.

Rod bent down to examine the ankle. "Try to stand. I think it's just a sprain."

Two of the younger male dancers linked their hands together to make a sort of chair and carried her back to where we had left the van. Rod, white with anger or concern or both, didn't speak on the trip back, but as they entered the hotel, he shouted at the manager to call a doctor.

"Why did we ever come to this godforsaken country?" he asked no one in particular but seemed to be staring pointedly at Julia.

"Come on, kid, I'll buy you a drink," Harper said to Julia, who was feeling guilty and upset. "It wasn't your fault – she's just clumsy. And those ridiculous sandals! Anyway, luckily, she's not one of the dancers. In a way, it serves her right. Wasn't she the one who insisted on coming to Angkor?"

The next day, Mrs. Lupino limped gamely around on a cane. Harper had arranged to have flowers sent to her with a card supposedly signed by the Ambassador, and she was all smiles.

"You really are a diplomat," Julia chided him, but gratefully.

When dusk fell, the VIPs, including the Prince, high government officials and the diplomatic corps, waited in the seats that had been set up in the courtyard, while hundreds of ordinary Cambodians sat on the ground around the moat. The rains, fortunately, had held off, but their threatening presence made the air heavy with heat and humidity. The elaborately dressed guests used the silk fans the Embassy had laid on each chair not only to dispel the oppressive heat but as weapons against marauding mosquitoes.

"And to think we could have held this in the air-conditioned comfort of the Salle des Conferences in Phnom Penh," Harper said to Julia, who barely heard him. She was looking longingly at Hourani, who was with a luminously beautiful Denise.

As the spotlight focused on the dancers, who stood on the terrace of intricately carved sandstone, the audience began to quiet. Music blared from the sound system, and the performance began.

The appearance and demeanor of the dancers stood in stark contrast to the spectacular setting and seemed to baffle the audience so used to the color and pageantry of Cambodian ballet. The American performers wore black tights and leotards, the only color provided by red silk scarves, which they twisted and hurled at each other like weapons. In the last number, billed in the program as "The Death of the Emperor Jones," Rod stood center stage while another male dancer wound a scarf around his neck, like a noose. After a stylized struggle, Rod slid gracefully to the floor, and the other dancers threw their scarves around him, simulating a pool of blood.

The audience gasped, and there was a momentary silence. Then the Prince stood up and led the applause.

"Let's hope he slept through that last number," whispered Harper.

After the performance, the Prince gave Rod the Order of the Silver Buffalo, an ornate medal of Cambodian silver. It had never been bestowed on an American before, and the Ambassador grinned with pleasure, anticipating the triumph he could report to Washington. Back at the hotel, he bought champagne for the company and the Embassy staff and sat back puffing on a malodorous cigar.

"Telephone for Ambassador Braithwaite," announced a bellhop.

"Take it for me, will you Bill?" he said, turning to Harper. "I don't want to break up the party just yet."

A few minutes later, Harper returned to the room, ashen-faced, and whispered to the Ambassador. The call had come from the Embassy Duty Officer in Phnom Penh, Jake O'Donnell. Joan Pendleton, the Ambassador's secretary, was dead on arrival at the French Hospital, where she had been rushed by ambulance from Madame Phuong's.

Back in Phnom Penh the next day, the Embassy staff was in a state of shock, and no one read the editorial in *La Dépêche* until mid-afternoon. The left-leaning newspaper interpreted the last dance, which was based on a Eugene O'Neill play, as promoting regicide. The dancing rebel who put the noose around the emperor's neck, said the editorial was a stand-in for Sihanouk's nemesis, Son Ngoc Thanh.

"Perhaps the Americans are using the dance as a signal to their puppet that the time is ripe," concluded the editorialist.

"Of course it's absurd," said Harper at the hastily called staff meeting. "*La Dépêche* knows it's absurd. But Sihanouk is so paranoid he's likely to believe it. Didn't anybody in the Embassy vet these dances? Regicide is not exactly a popular theme here. Jesus!"

"Who the hell is Son Yuck Tan?" asked Rod when he was told about the editorial.

Thanh, of mixed Cambodian and Vietnamese blood, had been a member of the Viet Minh, an outspoken enemy of the French. During the war, he had worked with the Japanese and, after independence, when Sihanouk was king, Thanh briefly served as Premier, a sort of elder statesman to the young monarch –who later abdicated and became simply 'Chief of State.' But Sihanouk was jealous of Thanh's status as a freedom fighter, and soon exiled him. Thanh was believed to be living in the jungle in Thailand, leading an anti-Sihanouk underground movement called the Khmer Serei, the Free Khmers.

The Ambassador was determined that we should hold a press conference and have Rod deny that the dance had any political relevance, but Rod was balking.

"Can't we just say that we're artists who don't give a flying fuck about Cambodian politics?" he asked petulantly. "Before this tour, I couldn't have found Cambodia on a map. I only agreed to come here because my wife wanted to see Angkor Wat."

Charlie Sherman took Rod's part, probably because he didn't want to be bothered but ostensibly because "we don't want to get on the wrong side of *La Dépêche*."

"We're already on the wrong side," Harper pointed out, and in the end, Rod reluctantly agreed to speak at a press conference, and Sherman, rolling his eyes, directed his staff to grind out press releases and statements. Bottles of soda in bowls of ice were set up at one end of the Embassy conference room, and the reporters helped themselves, and then sat down.

The Ambassador introduced Rod, who mouthed the bland speech that had been written for him: "All of us in this troupe are enthralled by the beauty and intricacy of the Cambodian ballet and charmed by the warm hospitality of the Cambodian people. We have been granted a rare privilege, and we are grateful to have had the opportunity to share the glories of dance with the members of the Royal Cambodian Ballet and with the Cambodian nation. I am particularly honored to have been awarded the Order of the Silver Buffalo by Cambodia's revered leader, Prince Norodom Sihanouk."

The staff handed out copies of Rod's speech in French and Cambodian, but none of the reporters even glanced at them. When the Ambassador opened the floor to questions, Bo Samphieu, there to represent the *Phnom-Penh Presse*, raised his hand.

"In the Emperor Jones dance," he asked, "did you mean to justify the murder of a monarch?"

Abandoning the talking points they had prepared for him, Rod launched into a sermon on artistic freedom and art-for-art's-sake, which left the reporters puzzled, even after Ket had rendered it in French and Khmer.

"Why couldn't he just have said 'no'?" groaned Harper afterwards. "And the Ambassador's little speech about how O'Neill's emperor was really just an upstart probably made it worse. But at least nobody asked a question about Joan."

Next day, *La Dépêche* led with the headline: "American dancer declines to deny sympathetic portrayal of traitor Son Ngoc Thanh." The centrist *Phnom-Penh Presse* carried only a brief account of the press conference, focusing on Rod's praise of Cambodian dance and hospitality, plus, on page 16, an obituary for "Joan Pendleton, American Embassy Secretary," with the notation that "the cause of death was not reported."

Jour de Gloire

From Julia's journal – ... On the flight back from Siem Reap, my period came on quite suddenly. I almost cried to feel the last traces of Hourani washing from my body with such finality.... Harper saw I was depressed – though I don't think he knows why – and suggested I take up fencing. He used to fence at Princeton and told me about the fencing master attached to the French military mission...

"*Reculez! Reculez quand vous êtes menacée!*" shouted the fencing master. "Back up when you are threatened!"

Too late, Julia moved away from her opponent, a Chinese woman who had recently moved to Phnom Penh from Saigon and who was a much better fencer than Julia.

"*Touchée!*" yelled the fencing master. Her opponent's foil – women were only allowed to use foils, not *epées* or sabers – touched the "*zone valable*" on Julia's padded fencing vest. Though she was taller and had longer legs, Julia could not keep up with the petite, energetic woman, who soon scored four touches to Julia's one.

The humid heat in the salon – actually a third-floor apartment on the Boulevard Monivong cooled only by ceiling fans – was becoming unbearable, and Julia tipped her foil to her opponent and headed for the shower. She stripped off the vest, shorts, and sweat-soaked underwear and stood under the cold water until she felt energized again, then changed into the fresh clothes she had brought in her Pan Am flight bag. By the time she emerged from the dressing room, the others had left, and the fencing master, Robert Bouvelle, had changed into a short-sleeved shirt and neatly pressed khaki pants. His short, military-cut hair was freshly combed, and he smelled of cologne.

"*Est-ce que vous permettez que je vous invite à prendre un apéritif, mademoiselle?*" he asked. "May I invite you to drink an aperitif with me?"

Julia was surprised, as he had always been strictly business, and she suspected he had a wife back in France, but she was curious about him and reluctant to go home to her empty apartment, so she agreed. They climbed into his battered *Deux-Chevaux*, and he drove out the Boulevard, away from the city. The rain had stopped, but when the car reached the dirt road that led to *Petite Kep*, it was muddy with puddles and they had to proceed slowly. Frogs sent up a loud, atonal chant. Mangroves shrouded the shores of the Mekong, and the dense, lush canopy of trees made Julia feel as if they were miles from the capital.

"The road to Saigon – once you get near the border – is like this," he said. "It's almost impossible to drive there in the rainy season. But in the *saison fraîche*, you should come with us. We go in convoy, and there is no trouble. If the Viet Cong patrols stop us, we show them our French passports, and they wave us on. It's impossible to go to Hanoi, *malheureusement*. That was the best – *un petit Paris*. But Saigon has some ambiance. Not like Phnom Penh – this is a provincial backwater."

Julia had been to Saigon a couple of times but had always traveled by air. When she pointed out to Bouvelle that she had a U.S. passport, he shrugged and said that the Viet Cong rarely looked at the women's documents, but his enthusiasm was obviously cooling. The VC might well want to make an example of any French who were fellow travelers of the enemy, the Americans.

The old wooden boat – the *Maison Flottante* – was tied to some of the towering mango trees that lined the bank, and they sat at a table on the deck and ordered Cinzanos and sipped them slowly, hoping for a breeze from the river. He began talking in rapid French, but Julia barely heard him, remembering the first time she went to *Petite Kep*, late one night with Hourani. The *Maison Flottante* had already closed, but they woke up the bar boy, who lived there, and drank some cognac. Then they sent him to bed and made love on the deck under a starry sky. Afterward, they swam in the path the moon had painted on the dark river.

"A backwater – just like this little branch of the Mekong," Bouvelle was saying, becoming more melancholy with each sip of Cinzano. "France was once a great nation. We had our *mission civilatrice. Maintenant, c'est fini…*" he shrugged. "When I came home from Algeria, after the war, people spat on us in the street – French people. I couldn't live in France, so here I am. *C'est intéressant…*"

Misinterpreting the word, Julia spouted on about how interesting Cambodia was, the culture, the history, and he laughed.

"*C'est a` dire, c'est intérresant au point de vue financière,*" he clarified. "The money is good."

The sky had begun to darken, not only with approaching night but with impending rain, so he paid the bar boy, and they headed back to the city. In front of Julia's apartment building, he opened the car door and kissed her hand.

The next day, she received an engraved invitation to the Bastille Day celebration at the Mission Militaire Française, with a note saying he would be honored to escort her.

Like the American Fourth of July celebration, when overdressed guests had crowded a sweltering tent behind the Ambassador's residence, Bastille Day was heavy with heat and rain. Nevertheless, the French women were dressed quite formally, in silks and jewelry, and the men wore suits and ties or dress uniforms. There was a scattering of diplomats, some in native dress, and a number of upper class, French-educated Cambodians, whom Bouvelle referred to—condescendingly, Julia felt— as "*les petits évolués.*" Julia waved to the Marcellinis, seated at a table with other French civil servants. Most of the guests drank red wine from long tables holding opened bottles set in an open-sided tent. The heavy, unchilled wine seemed to intensify the heat, and added to the melancholy mood as old soldiers told tales of battles won and wars lost. Toward midnight, the rains came down, and, as if that were a signal, a group of officers lined up and sang *La Marseillaise.*

"*Allons, enfants de la patrie, le jour de gloire est arrivé…*"

But their faces said otherwise: The day of glory had clearly passed.

Les Débutantes de Bokor

From Julia's journal – We are busy at the office putting out brochures – in Khmer and French – about Martin Luther King's rally at the Lincoln Memorial. Charlie Sherman just wanted to ignore it. "Why wash our dirty laundry in public?" he asked at the staff meeting. "Besides, Cambodians don't care about race issues." I knew he was wrong. Students who had studied in the States told me they were "treated like Negroes," and Ang Khem said that when he went for military training in Alabama, he was told to stay on the base because "the locals might take you for a nigger." I pushed the brochure, so Charlie dumped all the work on me... Jake O'Donnell, as consular officer, has to take care of all the details of Joan's death, identifying the body and dealing with the coroner and with Joan's family. The coroner found she had died of a drug overdose – there were sleeping pills as well as a lot of alcohol and opium in her system. The official verdict was "accidental drug overdose," but, of course, there is the suspicion of suicide, which makes Jake feel terribly guilty. He is arranging to have her body shipped home for burial in the family plot in Connecticut...

Vietnamese women, who had traded their weekday costumes of black pajama pants and white blouses for Sunday-best pastel *hao dais* with flowing white trousers underneath, passed on bicycles, their dresses ballooning like sails in the soft breeze from the river. Jake barely seemed to notice them, a sure sign he wasn't his old self. He and Julia had been to Mass in the old Portuguese church in the Vietnamese quarter, and were walking back to town along the river, which was lined with neat houseboats, their decks covered with containers of growing vegetables.

"Let's stop for lunch," he proposed, and they crossed the gangplank to the Lotus d'Or, a riverboat-restaurant permanently tied up along the quay, and ordered a large platter of small crispy fried fish from the great lake north of the city. They sat by the rail, looking down at the ferry that crossed the river to the island of Churi Changwar and said little for a while. Then, over a second bottle of *Trent-Trois* beer, Jake told her what had happened to Joan's body.

"One of the forms I was supposed to fill out for the Department was a statement that the body was face-up in the coffin," he said. "I had to certify that it was. But I couldn't bear to look at Joan's dead body. I asked the undertaker, and he assured me that everything was in order, so I signed the paper. But when the casket arrived in the States, Joan's father insisted on opening it. The body was upside down, and Joan's face had been smashed to a pulpy mess."

The family had been furious and complained to the State Department – a very black mark on Jake's record.

"I don't give a damn about my career. It's already going to hell in a hand basket," he said. "But Joanie, Joanie … She loved me, you know. And the one thing I could have done for her—I let her down because I didn't have the guts to look at her corpse."

A tear ran down his cheek.

"Oh, Jake," she said. "The dead are dead. They don't suffer. You were good to her while she lived…"

"No, that's just it – I wasn't," he said. "I went to bed with Joanie when I first arrived. It was after a party, and we were both a little drunk. She isn't – wasn't – inexperienced, so I didn't think she'd take it seriously, but she did. I felt like a heel…"

There was nothing more Julia could say, so she gently placed her hand over his and tried to change the subject.

"Are you going to Hourani's birthday party?" she asked, probably too brightly and not quite looking him in the eye.

Since that night she had run into him as she left Hourani's bungalow for the first time, neither Julia nor Jake had talked about the affair. But, of course, Jake knew, and he knew it was over and that he had been right.

"I wasn't planning to, but I'll take you if you want to go," he offered, and Julia could have kissed him. She wanted to go but not alone. She told herself it would show that she didn't care, but deep down, she hoped he would see her and suddenly realize that he really loved her.

By the day of the party, the rains had ended, and the breeze off the river had turned from hot to almost cool. (In Harper's words, "Now that the rainy season is over it's just one goddamn beautiful day after another.") Like spring in the temperate zones, the beginning of the cooler, drier season seemed to signal a rebirth. The *cyclo* drivers quickened their pace, the tennis courts at the Cercle Sportif were more crowded, and at the Ancien Marché, the old market across the road from the river, you could buy raspberries and strawberries raised in the small hill station at Bokor. (The hill station also held Cambodia's first casino, a much-vaunted project built to attract hard currency – only foreigners could enter. Now it stood eerily empty, a monument to failure.) In contrast to the indoor Central Market – which was noisy, crowded and smelled of blood –the old, outdoor market was quiet and pleasant. At the outer perimeter sat bamboo cages with songbirds that could be liberated on Buddhist holidays, for a fee, to earn merit for the liberator. Late at night, Julia and her friends would often stop at the market for a bowl of *soupe chinoise* –noodle soup with shrimp, crab and chicken topped with coriander leaves and anise stars and laced with *tuk trei*, the Cambodian version of *nguoc mam*, an odiferous fermented fish sauce. She could smell the boiling soup that night as they pulled up beside the market in Jake's car.

"I'll just be a minute," she said, stepping onto the sidewalk.

At the flower stall, Julia looked at containers filled with waxy red anthuriums, vibrant birds-of-paradise, cerise hibiscus flowers, blowsy orange blooms that looked something like gladioli, but a bouquet of rosebuds caught her eye.

"*Les débutantes de Bokor, mademoiselle* – rosebuds just arrived from the hill station," the vendor urged.

The tiny pink-red buds were straining against the hard green membrane, showing just their bursting tips, but the smell was strong. Julia hadn't seen or smelled roses since she left the States, and the bouquet made her nostalgic for colder climes with more subtle, less flamboyant flowers than she knew here. She quickly purchased them, and the vendor wrapped them in one of the Embassy pamphlets on the civil rights march, she noted sheepishly. She held the bouquet near her face as they rode across the city to the Royale, savoring the heady smell, almost tempted to keep the flowers.

Hourani was standing at the door of the already crowded bungalow, and Julia handed him the bouquet and whispered, *"Bon anniversaire, chéri."*

He took her hand and quickly released it, embarrassed – Denise was watching him with a proprietorial air. Julia felt odd to be there among all these people in this place so filled with memories of intimacy. When the dancing started, she knew she couldn't bear to watch Hourani dancing with Denise, so she asked Jake to take her home.

Instead, they went to the Bar Jean, across the road from the river, next to the Ancien Marché, and sat at the bar under a sign that read *"Vin gratuit demain"* (always tomorrow), and ate *soupe a l'oignon gratinée*, and played blackjack with the genial Jean while his Vietnamese mistress tended bar (all the while keeping a close eye on Jean – she was said to be jealous). When they got back to Julia's apartment, Jake took her in his arms and kissed her tenderly, and she knew that he had appreciated the gift of the roses, even if Hourani hadn't.

Perhaps, in a sense, the flowers – and the gesture – had been meant for him, she thought, and she was tempted to ask him to stay, and as his kisses became more urgent, she knew he would have agreed. Then she thought of Jake's fiancée back home – the one who was saving herself for marriage – and of poor dead Joan, and she pushed him gently away and knew from his eyes that he understood.

Le Destinataire

*From Julia's journal –The Khmer Serei have begun
clandestine anti-Sihanouk, pro-Son Nguoc Thanh
broadcasts from a secret location, presumably in Thailand.
The Prince has accused the CIA of backing this group,
so relations are in a tailspin. There are rumors that Bo
Samphieu is a Khmer Serei operative and, since he has
an American wife – and, now, a half-American son – that
adds to the anti-American feelings. I went to a dinner at
the Public Affairs Officer's house last evening, and the
two Cambodian officials who had been invited sent last
minute regrets... Coming home from the Embassy today,
I noticed a large gathering outside the Buddhist temple
down the street. Buddhist monks are burning themselves
to death in Saigon to protest the Diem regime, and the
monks here are demonstrating to show solidarity. They
blame us, of course, which probably explains why the
young bonzes from the temple never come by to practice
English and drink Pepsi Cola anymore. Even if they
did, I doubt that they'd say, "America good."*

Julia was just home from her Saturday swim at the Cercle Sportif (she had started going to the Cercle late in the day when Hourani wasn't likely to be there) when the Embassy jeep pulled up. She was the Embassy Duty Officer that weekend, but only rarely did anything of importance happen, and she had forgotten to tell the *boyesse* where she was going. Lanh was pacing about, looking nervous.

"He come before," she said. "I tell him you back soon."

Luckily, it was nothing urgent. The driver said there was a cable for a visiting journalist that had to be picked up at the Post Office because it was marked "*les frais doivent s'e tre payé par le destinataire.*" In other words, the cable had come collect. It was up to Julia to find the addressee, one Peter Stein.

She rode to the Embassy with the driver, took some money out of petty cash, picked up the cable at the Post Office and set off on a search of likely hotels. He wasn't at the Mondial or the Hôtel de la Poste or the Maharajah – the budget hotels where journeymen journalists usually stayed—so she tried the Royale and found him at the bar. She turned away to give him some privacy while he read the cable, then asked if he needed a ride to the Post Office or anywhere.

"No, thanks," he said, "but you'd be doing me a big favor if you'd have a drink with me. I've had bad news, though I won't burden you with it."

He was tall and lean with a handsome but care-worn face and blue eyes that looked directly at her.

"All right," she agreed.

She dismissed the driver, and they carried their drinks outside and sat on the terrace under the mango trees.

"What brings you to Phnom Penh?" she asked. There was little real news here, so big-name journalists rarely visited. Viet Nam was the story.

"I'm trying to get an interview with Sihanouk," he explained. "I want to write about the difference between Cambodia and Viet Nam – not just the usual crap about the contrast between war-torn Viet Nam and peaceful Cambodia but trying to dig a little deeper – looking into how the history and leadership of the two countries are determining their fates. But I'm probably boring you. I'm sorry."

"Not at all," she protested. "I'm fascinated. The Embassy people seem to treat Sihanouk as a joke – or a madman."

"Crazy like a fox," he said and told her about Viet Nam, which he had been covering for years. Then they ordered a second round of drinks and he told her what the cable had said: His wife was leaving Hong Kong for London, where there were better schools for their son.

"It also happens to be where her boyfriend lives," he said dryly, and she recognized a fellow victim of lost love and didn't have the heart to tell him his wife had sent the cable collect.

Next day, he stopped by Julia's office after his interview with Ambassador Braithwhite and Tom Grant.

"I wondered if you'd help me with some translations. Your French is so good," he said. "And perhaps you'd let me buy you dinner in return."

"It's part of my job to help journalists," she said. "You don't have to buy me dinner."

"Please, I'd like to," he answered, and she knew she'd like it too.

She translated some of Sihanouk's speeches and part of an old French book on Indochina, and they started having dinner several nights a week in offbeat places in the *quartier chinois*. Often, they'd end the evening with a cooling swim in the pool at the Hotel Royal. "My mermaid," he called her.

Once, she led him to one of the simple, clean Vietnamese restaurants clustered around the Phnom – the park-like temple grounds shaded by tall plane trees. In the center of the park stood the small hill where a woman named Penh had once lived, giving the city its name. After eating the traditional vermicelli flavored with coriander and *nguoc mam* and washing it down with Vietnamese beer, they walked up the stone path laced with banyan roots to the temple and watched the astrologers reading their complex charts to customers by the light of kerosene lamps.

"Do you believe in all that – that our fate is written in the stars?" he asked her, only half in jest as they walked down the hill, stepping over the giant, gnarled roots on the banyan tree.

"No – not really," she answered. "But if I spoke enough Cambodian, I might listen to what they had to say."

"Astrology's important here," he said. "And maybe the people who believe in it are right. So much seems to depend on chance, but maybe it *is* written in the stars – or somewhere. If my wife hadn't sent me that telegram, if you hadn't been on duty that day, we might never have met…"

He looked into her eyes, then laughed.

"Enough of my crazy thoughts," he said. "Come on – I'll take you home."

When he got word that the Prince had agreed to an interview, Julia was glad for him but a little sad. Did that mean he'd leave Phnom Penh? She realized she'd miss their time together. She was happier when she was with him, happier than she'd been since the break-up with Hourani, and when he looked at her with those intense blue eyes, something stirred deep within her – something she had thought was dead. But he was married, however unhappily.

"Sihanouk is earthy and smart," he said as they had dinner the night after the interview. "I interviewed Diem last month, and it was like talking to a zombie. He's in a mystical world all his own. He's an egomaniac who believes he's anointed by God and not the god most of his people follow. If South Viet Nam had a leader like Sihanouk, they'd have beaten the Communists long ago."

One night he seemed rather quiet, and over drinks in the bar at the Maharajah Hotel after dinner, he told her his wife had asked him for a divorce.

"Being a foreign correspondent is hard on a marriage," he said. "So is the Foreign Service. Probably the best thing for you would be to go home, marry your college sweetheart, and settle down in Scarsdale."

"But not yet, please, not yet," he added with a grin.

Fête des Eaux

From Julia's journal – I asked Lanh to go to Michaud, the French provisioner, to buy the paté and cheeses for the party I'm giving for the Fête des Eaux, but she looked stricken and finally said, "Please, mademoiselle, they make fun of me there. Please, you go." Apparently, the French clerks there mock the choppy, sing-song way most Vietnamese speak French. So, I went myself, and if they tittered at my American accent, it wasn't until after I was out of earshot... Every year at the end of the rainy season, on a date fixed by the Palace astrologer, Cambodians celebrate the Festival of the Reversing Current, usually just called the Fête des Eaux. Here's how the official guidebook describes it: "Phnom Penh sits at the confluence of the Mekong, the Tonle Sap and the Bassac rivers. From this point, the intermingled rivers flow into small tributaries and filter down through the swampy delta of South Viet Nam into the South China Sea. During the summer, the monsoon rains—coupled with melting snow from the Himalayas way upstream – threaten to overwhelm the tributary streams, and nature provides a solution. The Mekong waters rush down with such force that they cause the waters of the Tonle Sap to reverse direction and flow upstream, into the vast, shallow Grand Lac. The lake overflows and floods the plain. When the rains cease, the flood subsides, leaving rich, rice-nurturing soil and marooning fish on the branches of low-hanging trees. As the water level lowers, the flow of the river returns to normal, and the Mekong again flows downstream, into the delta and then to the sea."

The river breeze stirred the air on the royal barge, and the Prince strutted up and down the deck in a ceremonial silk costume, greeting guests effusively, even the Americans. Despite the increasingly virulent Khmer Serei broadcasts and a consequent step-up in Sihanouk's anti-American rants, the Prince had invited most of the Embassy staff to view the races and the parade from his graciously appointed boat. Julia sat on the open deck with Ket, the young Embassy translator who was the closest thing she had to a girlfriend. Crowds lined the riverbank as far as the eye could see, and there was a hum of excitement that sometimes erupted into loud cheers for various pirogue boats, which were racing each other up the river to a finish line in front of the barge.

"The people come not only to cheer the boats, but to pay their respects to the life-giving spirit of the waters," explained Ket, who was wearing traditional Cambodian dress for the occasion – a rose-colored lace blouse over a long, sarong-like silk skirt. "The pirogues are painted in the colors of their villages. The silk tassels on the front of the boats are meant to keep away evil spirits … Oh, it looks like the ceremony is about to start. *Monseigneur* is about to cut the string to release the water… Symbolically, he is commanding the river to reverse its current, to flow back toward the sea again."

"You didn't know he had magic powers, did you?" asked Harper, who had come up behind us. "Next, he's going to walk on water."

"Oh, *Monsieur* Harper," Ket said in mock horror. "*Vous blaguez.* You are joking."

"Are you saying I am *pas sérieux*?" he retorted, teasing her.

"No," Julia chimed in, "just irreverent."

He should probably warn Julia about Ket, he thought. They were too close, and Julia was young and naïve. He had once run into Ket coming out of the Ministry of Foreign Affairs. She had looked embarrassed and stammered something about her mother's passport, but he had no doubt that she was an informant. She wasn't supposed to have access to classified documents, but some of the Embassy people were sloppy. And she was a notorious gossip. She had probably told the Ministry about Julia's affair with the Moroccan playboy. Not blackmail material, but still...

Their banter was drowned out as the parade of boats, trailing the colorful streamers of their villages, began passing the Prince's reviewing stand, to the thunderous cheers of the crowds on the bank. Last to file past was the winning boat, which approached the Prince's barge. Sihanouk leaned over the side and threw flowers into the pirogue, then gave the captain a trophy – to more tumultuous cheering.

After that, the festivities on the barge turned into just another cocktail party. Ornately dressed Palace servants passed trays of soft drinks and beer, and the guests waited, none too patiently, for the Prince to leave so they could make their own departures without breaking protocol.

Julia would have liked to linger for the fireworks, but she was giving a party that night so, as soon as Sihanouk and his entourage walked up the gangplank, she and Ket left, too. They walked through the darkening streets to the small second-floor apartment Ket shared with her widowed mother and her younger sister. Her mother had made some Cambodian sweets for the party – sticky rice cakes encased in banana leaves and some kind of pastries rolled in grated coconut. They were sitting on two silver trays beautifully decorated with flowers. Julia thanked her profusely and reiterated her invitation to the party, but she again declined. Her late husband, she explained, had been *chef de cabinet*, or chief of staff, in the Ministry of Agriculture, and when he was alive, they had frequently attended social functions.

"*Mais, maintenant, c'est fini*," she shrugged. "That's over now."

The social suttee of Cambodian widows.

"*Allons, on est pressé*," said Ket, eager to be away. "We need to hurry."

They hailed two *cyclos* and carefully balanced the trays on their laps. When they arrived at Julia's building, all the usual street vendors had temporarily abandoned their wares and were lined up at the edge of the terrace, watching the preparations. Lanh had pressed several other *boyesses* into service, and they bustled about in their long, silky black pants, arranging flowers, polishing trays, putting ice in buckets. Julia gave the trays of sweets to Lanh, who placed them on the buffet. The long dining room table was laden with cheese, pâté, shrimp, a whole baked fish, cucumber salad, and plates of sliced fruits, all under mosquito netting until the guests arrived.

Julia put some long-playing records on the stereo and took a quick shower. She had just changed into a dress she had had made of Cambodian silk when the guests became to filter in, and the party took on a life of its own. There were Cambodian, French, and other diplomatic guests, as well as many from the American community, and people danced to pop music and jazz.

"You're quite the hostess," said Peter Stein. He steered her into the living room, which was crowded with people dancing and talking. Charlie Sherman, who must have started drinking before the party came up to them and slurred,"I see young Julia's already taking over my job of liaising with the press."

Peter ignored him.

"Let's dance," he said to Julia.
.

Charlie's wife, Betty, looking very uncomfortable, pleaded with Charlie to go home, but he shouted at her and threw a highball glass on the marble floor.

"What an asshole," said Peter.

Lanh moved swiftly to clean up the broken glass, and few of the guests even glanced at the Shermans. Across the room, Magda Blair was flirting with a newly arrived young attaché from the Australian Embassy, standing so close that her breasts periodically brushed his shirt.

"Magda has a new one in her clutches," Julia whispered to Peter.

"Don't be too hard on her, darling," he said, looking at Magda with a mixture of sorrow and empathy. "She's getting old, and this is her way of clinging to youth, of squeezing the last drop out of life. Maybe that's why I can't keep away from you – you're so young and fresh."

"You're not old," she protested, noticing for the first time a few gray hairs at his temples.

"I'm forty-six – twice as old as you," he said.

"But you won't always be," she said and immediately regretted her words, which implied that they had a future together. She mustn't be possessive. She knew now that was why she had lost Hourani.

"I can't promise you a future," he said, lifting her chin and forcing her to look directly into his eyes. "But there's a chemistry between us, and it's not just physical. I think you want it as much as I do. We'll be good for each other, and I'll try to make sure you don't get hurt."

Julia stepped back for a moment and looked up at him. She hadn't thought she could fall in love again so quickly, but as he pulled her close and kissed her ear, her breath came faster and faster, and she ran her fingers up and down the hair on his forearms and there may as well have been no one else in the room.

About two hours into the party, Tom Grant arrived with the news that there had been a military coup that afternoon in Saigon.

"Diem and his brother, Nhu, are in hiding," Tom said, although he suspected they might have been assassinated.

Everyone clustered around Grant, trying to get more details, but he knew – or said – little, other than the official line: that the U.S. government had no foreknowledge of or role in the coup.

With that news, the mood of the party became jubilant, especially among the Americans, who had considered Diem a roadblock in the effort to win the hearts and minds of the people. But Lanh, a Catholic and a refugee from North Viet Nam, overheard some of the French guests discussing the coup and began to cry hysterically in a corner, squatting on the floor and muttering, "*Moi catholique, moi catholique*. They killed him. They will kill all the Catholics."

Julia tried to comfort her and told her not to worry because now things would go better for Viet Nam—that the war would be won and the Communists defeated. But Lanh refused to be comforted, looking at Julia with wiser, sadder eyes, a Cassandra crying knowingly amidst the jubilation.

Peter had his notebook out and was talking to some of the Embassy people and to the editor of the Phnom-Penh Presse. He grabbed Julia's hand as she walked by and handed her a note: "Come back to the hotel with me. We can go for a swim in the pool, and I have to make arrangements to get back to Saigon."

She felt guilty leaving her own party but it was winding down and she decided that, with all the excitement and the liquor, no one would miss her and she wanted more than anything else in the world to be alone with him. She went to the bedroom and grabbed a bathing suit and they left quickly, sharing a *cyclo*, and she could barely keep her hands off him as they glided through the quiet streets to the Royale.

"Whatever harm the French did with their colonial policies," he remarked, gazing admiringly at the well laid out streets lined with majestic trees, "they certainly knew how to build cities."

He stopped at the hotel desk to book a morning flight, then they headed outside to the pool, which was empty of people, its neon-blue waters glowing harshly in the soft-coal blackness of the night. Lights from the bar illumined scattered green patches on the lawn, and a soft breeze ruffled the bougainvillea vines that climbed the hotel.

They swam for a while and floated on their backs and looked up at the stars. Finally, they got cold and wrapped themselves in the plush hotel towels and climbed the grand staircase to his room and the big bed swathed in mosquito netting.

Julia liked it that they talked while they made love, and even laughed. With Hourani, lovemaking had been silent, almost solemn. She ran her thumb along the hard ridge of his forehead and murmured, "I love your eyebrows." He moved them up and down two or three times in a sort of Groucho Marx imitation and asked, "Is that all?"

She laughed, and then, her throat too full for speech, silently enumerated all the other things about him she was learning to love.

Next morning at dawn, Julia took a *cyclo* home, and Peter took a cab to the airport to board the first plane to Saigon.

Lam Ton, Interrupted

From Julia's journal – Letter from Peter: "Come to Saigon, darling, so we can make love under the mosquito netting in my big bed at the Continental. When I get the piece about the coup wrapped up, we can fly up to Dalat in the mountains. It reminds me of the Adirondacks, where I went to camp as a kid. There's an American consulate there, and on the night of the coup, the consul, a gutsy young guy, broke into Madame's Nhu's compound and pissed in her pool." Meanwhile, things here in Phnom Penh remain tense. Though we thought the coup in Saigon would improve our relations with Cambodia, the opposite seems to be true. Concluding that the U.S. had backed the move against Diem, Sihanouk apparently fears he will be the next victim. If the Americans so cavalierly disposed of their faithful puppet, he reasons, what wouldn't they do to him?

The Café Mozart was on the outskirts of town, near the raw, new section known only as "Kilomètre Six," and Ang Khem's Peugeot negotiated the potholes slowly.

"I have a surprise for you," the young officer said shyly. "I have taken dancing lessons."

Julia remembered the night at the hotel in Kep when he had danced with Denise Foletti. Like Julia, he had been stiff and awkward, and it had been as if Denise and Hourani had been the only dancers on the floor. She shuddered at the memory of the night she had begun to lose him. It still hurt.

"Ah, but I haven't," she said. "You will have to dance with one of the taxi girls."

At the Café Mozart, couples could go to dance in the large, airy pavilion, but there were also taxi dancers for men who came alone. The women weren't prostitutes, but, Jake had told her, some of them later "graduated" to bars like the Chez Tyna, where more than dancing was expected of them.

Ang Khem laughed.

"You'll be fine. You're a good dancer," he assured her.

They found a table and ordered *café liégois*, and to Julia's relief, the band struck up a *Lam Ton*, a uniquely Cambodian dance that was a combination of a conga line and the Bunny Hop, which had been popular when she was in college. This, she could do, and she let Ang

Khem lead her onto the already crowded floor. They got behind some people he seemed to know, and she followed them, moving her arms in a sort of loose imitation of the Cambodian ballet dancers. The line went faster and faster, and the high-pitched, almost hypnotic music got louder and louder. Then, abruptly, it stopped. The dancers looked around, puzzled.

The manager came to the microphone and announced, solemnly, that Samdech Sahacavin – the folksy designation for Sihanouk – would address the nation on the radio. He turned the radio on, and the crowd clapped politely, although most of the people around her looked disappointed.

She sipped her coffee slowly as the Prince's voice got very loud and seemed to reach a feverish pitch. She couldn't understand what he was saying so she tuned out, but, after a while, she noticed that people were staring at her, looking embarrassed. Ang Khem lowered his eyes. She wanted to ask him what the Prince was saying, but she knew she couldn't. Finally, it was over, and the radio played the Cambodian National Anthem, and everyone stood. The band looked like it was going to reassemble, but Julia wanted to leave, and she suspected Ang Khem did, too.

"Please," she said. "I have a terrible headache."

He made small talk as they drove through the quiet streets, avoiding her inquisitive gaze, and pulled away quickly as soon as he had opened the car door for her outside her apartment building.

The next morning, she learned what the Prince had taken two hours to say: that America was his enemy and that he would henceforth dispense with all American aid – military, economic, and cultural aid.

"He'll never give up American aid," scoffed Charlie Sherman at the morning meeting.

"Famous last words," muttered Bill Harper.

Feu Le Président

From Julia's journal – Two sinister happenings – unrelated but somehow ominous. The CIA Station Chief came home for lunch one day last week and found – in his shower -- the dead body of a Cambodian agent he had recruited. He had invited the Japanese commercial officer to lunch that day and received him as if nothing had happened. Sang-froid. His maid, understandably hysterical about the body, had neglected to prepare the meal. But never mind. She calmed down and borrowed the lunch from another maid down the block. ...A few days later, Jean, the popular proprietor of the Bar Jean was found murdered. Rumors flew around Phnom Penh like shrill birds. Some whispered that it was the CIA, but it turned out he was shot by his jealous Vietnamese mistress...

"*Mademoiselle, mademoiselle,*" Lanh gently but insistently touched Julia's shoulder. The maid was clutching a piece of paper.

It was about 7 o'clock on a Saturday morning and she had gone to a party the night before and had planned to sleep late, but when she read the note, she woke up instantly.

"The President has been assassinated in Dallas," the note read, "Please come to the office."

She dressed quickly and walked to the curb, where an Embassy car was waiting with some of her colleagues already in it. They barely spoke as they rode to the Embassy.

"Dallas – some damn right-wing nut," said Harper between clenched teeth.

At the Embassy, people gathered around the teletype machine in the press office. Pulling off an eyewitness account of the assassination by Merimam Smith of UPI, Charlie Sherman, the Press Officer, curled his lip in distaste.

"Look at this," he said. "It's so sensational – disgusting."

"It's great reporting," countered Harper, reading it over Charlie's shoulder. "Smith will win a Pulitzer."

Kennedy died on Friday afternoon, but because of the time difference and the slowness of communication, the Embassy didn't learn of the tragedy until Saturday morning.

"In this backwater, even the news comes secondhand," said Harper bitterly. "Further proof of how little we matter."

But there was no time for bitterness or tears. The Embassy staff had to get the word out that the nation would go on, that our policy toward Cambodia would not change.

"Get your Cambodian staff in," ordered the Ambassador. "I don't care if it's a Saturday. The man who paid their salaries is dead."

Most of the Cambodian employees came in voluntarily when they heard the news, as dazed and grief-stricken as the Americans. When Than Meas from the exhibits section put up the photomontage of Kennedy's presidency in the Embassy window, his cheeks were streaked with tears. The staff worked like automatons all that day, digging into files to find pictures and quotes, grinding out press releases in French and Khmer about "feu le président" – the late President – and about the peaceful succession (especially needed after the headline in the leftist *La Dépêche* read "*Coup en Amerique?*")

"Can't we find a better picture of Johnson than that?" asked the Ambassador when he saw the photos for the quick brochure they were putting together.

Unfortunately, the only available photo of regional interest showed the Texan towering over the now dead Diem, and the only LBJ quotes about Southeast Asia professed staunch support of Cambodia's enemies – South Viet Nam and Thailand.

Anti-American signs came down, and the Ambassador received condolences from Sihanouk himself. The Prince had admired Kennedy – not least of all because, unlike Eisenhower, Kennedy had accorded Sihanouk VIP treatment on his visit to Washington. Sihanouk thought of Kennedy as a young, progressive, handsome leader – much like himself.

With a new regime in Saigon, the Buddhist monks there had stopped their self-immolations, and the bonzes next door came to Julia's apartment door with a bouquet of flowers. "For Kennedy," the leader said.

The American community was in official mourning, so they didn't have to worry about being shunned socially by Cambodians. And Cambodians could invite Americans to parties and functions without fear that they would accept and cause the hosts political discomfort. When Ket invited Julia to the birthday party she was giving

for a mutual friend, Julia pleaded official mourning and
Ket seemed relieved.

Meetings in Hell

*From Julia's journal –When we stopped by the Grants'
to pick up Tom that terrible morning, Sheila had been
standing by the door, her arms crossed in front of her
chest. Later, Tom told me that when he woke Sheila to
tell her what had happened, she pouted: "Every time
we plan a Saturday trip to the beach, something like this
has to happen." ...Peter wrote that on that Saturday
morning, Armed Forces Radio Saigon signed on about
five to seven, and the corporal in charge announced:
"In five minutes we'll have the news – and, boy, do we
have news for you this morning. But first, five minutes
of jazz." ...Memorial gifts are beginning to flood the
Embassy, and I seem to be in charge of them. Today
I received a portrait of the late President – an eerie
likeness executed in chicken feathers.*

Sihanouk was slated to broadcast another speech to
the nation that night, and Jake O'Donnell, as one of
the few Cambodian language officers at the post, was
assigned to listen and report on it. True, the Embassy

would receive the official translation the next day, but official translations were highly sanitized versions of the Prince's earthy rants and the Ambassador wanted a report on what he had really said, first thing in the morning. Jake had asked his maid to prepare an early dinner and planned to stay glued to his radio the rest of the evening. Then he got a message from Nicole.

After Chuck had left for his new posting in Manila, Nicole had remained at the Chez Tyna and resumed her old life, looking sadder yet wiser as the weeks passed without word from her Marine lover. She began going home with customers again, even with Jake a couple of times, crying on his shoulder before they went to bed. Then, much to Jake's surprise, Nicole had good news.

"I have received a letter from Chuck," she told him. "He asks that I come to Manila. Soon he will be discharged. Then we will marry."

She wanted Jake's help with the paperwork, and, of course, he agreed, then asked her, "Will you take the children?"

Nicole had a son and daughter by a resident Frenchman who had returned home.

She shook her head sadly, a bit defensively.

"I cannot – not yet, anyway. You know, he is younger than me," she confided. "The children will stay with my sister. She has agreed."

The night he was assigned to monitor Sihanouk's speech, Jake stopped at the bar after work in response to Nicole's message. She looked almost ill – she was pregnant, she confessed. She didn't know whether it was Chuck's baby, she said. After all, she didn't think she would ever see him again when he left, and she had to live, didn't she?

And even if it turned out to be Chuck's, a baby would be too much for him, at first, she continued. He was so young, and his family was very straight-laced. No, she said firmly, she had arranged to have an abortion. A girlfriend was supposed to take her to the clinic, in Kompong Speu, but her car had broken down.

Jake swallowed hard. But it couldn't have been his, he decided, relieved. He had always used a condom. The Embassy doctor had a stash he issued to bachelors at the post – geographical and others – accompanied by a stern lecture.

She looked desperate, so of course, Jake said he would drive her. He figured he would drop her there, come back and listen to the speech and go back to get her later. But when they arrived at the clinic, he knew he couldn't leave her. It was like a bad movie. The doctor had whisky on his breath, and the place was full of flies. He tried to talk her out of the whole thing, but she was determined, so he sat down on the porch and waited, watching the chickens scratch around the scruffy yard. After about an hour, the doctor came out and said it was over and that she could go but she should lie down.

"If she bleeds too much," he shrugged, "take her to a hospital."

Jake carried Nicole to the car and laid her down on the back seat and drove slowly, avoiding the potholes, back to Phnom Penh and to her room on the outskirts of the city. He sat beside her bed all night, holding her hand, and by morning the bleeding had stopped. He made rice and tea on her hot plate, and she ate and drank a little, and told him to go home.

Jake was so tired he forgot about Sihanouk's speech. When he did remember, it was too late. In any case, he assumed it had just been the same old diatribe and that the official translation would suffice.

Members of the Embassy staff gathered around the conference table in the Ambassador's office, their faces buried in the official translation (into French) of Sihanouk's latest speech.

"Just another *tour d'horizon* of his warped worldview," pronounced Harper.

"Maybe," said Ambassador Braithwhite, "but the Prince went on for almost three hours, and his translation is only five pages long. Who was supposed to be listening to the speech?"

"O'Donnell," said Tom Grant.

"Well, where the hell was O'Donnell? Where the hell is O'Donnell?" asked Braithwhite.

Tom picked up a phone and dialed Jake's extension at the consulate, but it was busy.

"I'll go get him," he volunteered, happy for a momentary escape from the Ambassador's ire. As he returned with a red-eyed, disheveled Jake in tow, one of the communications staff members came into the conference room and handed the Ambassador a cable from Washington. As he read it, he turned alternately pale and bright red.

"GO IMMEDIATELY – REPEAT, IMMEDIATELY – TO SIHANOUK AND DEMAND APOLOGY FOR BARBARIC SPEECH. RUSK."

Attached to that terse message was a copy of the unofficial translation, as monitored by the CIA listening post in Hong Kong. It was the ending of this long, bawdy hysterical invective that attracted everyone's attention.

"The enemies of Cambodia," Sihanouk had gloated, "are dying like flies."

First Diem, then Thailand's dictator Marshal Sarit – who had died of natural causes – and, then, "the big boss."

"The three enemies of Cambodia," he'd added gleefully, "can now conduct their SEATO meetings in Hell."

The Ambassador glared at Jake, practically sputtering.

"Thanks to you, we got caught with our pants down. We should have known about the speech first, so we could have reported it to Washington and put it in some perspective," he raged. "I don't see how your career, which was not star-quality to begin with, can survive two instances of neglect of duty in one tour – first the coffin mishap and now this."

"I'm sorry," Jake stammered but offered no explanation.

Nicole recovered quickly. She hadn't been very far along, which meant that the baby hadn't been Chuck's.

She left for Manila on schedule. Jake drove her to the airport.

"Jake is finished. He'll be allowed to resign for personal reasons and go home with his tail between his legs," Harper told Julia, not unsympathetically. "And all because Samdech fucking Sihanouk is one on a diet cures that drives him deeper into paranoia. I just hope Washington doesn't overreact. If the Ambassador had any courage, he'd tell them that. But he's just a sniveling errand boy. Why can't we be more like the French? When the Prince attacked them in a speech last month, their Ambassador went to the Foreign Ministry and complained – quietly. When the official translation came out, all the anti-French stuff had been expunged. Crisis over. This is a society where it's the façade that matters. Why can't we accept that?"

But while the Ambassador hemmed and hawed and tried to get an appointment with the Prince, in Washington – in a city and a country stunned with grief – the Cambodian Ambassador was summoned to the State Department and read the riot act by an official who called Sihanouk's speech "barbaric."

"As if that wasn't bad enough," said Harper, "the American official was only of ambassadorial rank. According to diplomatic protocol – and the Cambodians are sticklers for protocol – an Assistant Secretary of

State is the lowest ranking official fit to deal with an ambassador, who's the personal representative of a head of state. Another gratuitous insult hurled at hypersensitive Cambodia."

Post-Mortem

From Julia's journal –I looked for him every day, but finally heard from Peter—mail service between the two neighboring countries is inexplicably slow -- that he is not going to join the newsmen flocking to Phnom Penh, at least not for now. He is reporting on the workings of the fledgling government in Saigon, and what effect it will have on the success of the war against the Viet Cong. He is upbeat, and very happy that my transfer to Saigon has come through – I will go right after Christmas, in just a few weeks. I'll be sad to leave, but, more than anything, I want to be with Peter. I don't know whether we have a future, and I don't care. We're in love, and that's all I really need.

"Welcome to Never-Never Land," said Charlie Sherman, ushering an American television crew into the office.

The reporter grimaced, already sick of Charlie and his chumminess and his clichés. The cameraman, sweating

127

under his heavy equipment, just kept chewing his gum, his expression blank.

"Charlie is in heaven. Finally, he has some important journalists to drink with," said Harper. "If they can stand it. I guess that's why he leaked the full text of Sihanouk's speech to AP, which is going to cause us no end of trouble."

The influx of American journalists was putting a strain on the Embassy. The Ambassador and the political officers were giving briefings and interviews to them, trying to put things "in perspective," but the newsmen were having none of it.

"Perspective doesn't work on TV," one said bluntly. "It's too long for the public's attention span."

Tired of Embassy babysitting, most of the reporters hired their own guides and interpreters and combed the city doing "man-on-the-street" interviews. As Julia walked into the office, she saw cameras set up in front of the photomontage about Kennedy in the Embassy's front window.

"Get me some locals," the reporter barked to his guide.

In a few minutes, the guide returned with two young boys who had been selling cigarettes at a stand on the corner.

"Are you sad about President Kennedy's death?" the newsman asked.

As the interpreter translated, the boys looked into the television camera – something they had never seen before – and broke into toothy grins. They both nodded, then giggled nervously.

"Following the lead of their mercurial leader, Prince Norodom Sihanouk," the reporter intoned, "Cambodians I spoke to in their capital, Phnom Penh, were either indifferent to or jubilant about JFK's death…"

Washington reacted to the coverage emotionally, sending a sharp protest to the Cambodians that again used the word "barbaric."

"Barbaric?" sniffed an editorial in the heretofore friendly *Phnom-Penh Presse*, "and this from people whose ancestors lived in caves while ours ruled over a glorious civilization at Angkor."

Sihanouk restated with greater vehemence his intention to rid his country of all American aid.

Réveillon

From Julia's journal —Mary, Bo Samphieu's wife, came to my door last night, red-eyed from crying. Bo has disappeared, along with the so-called cousin who had been living with them — everyone assumed she's his mistress. He left no note for Mary, who is now alone with their small son, Rama — named for the hero of the Ramayana. Rumors are rife that Bo has joined the Khmer Serei in the jungle...

At 6 o'clock on Christmas Eve, the *quartier chinois* was filled with people darting across the narrow streets from shop to shop. Music blared in Chinese, French, and English from the record and stereo stores. Sidewalk dentists, fortunetellers, tea and soup vendors squatted on the sidewalk, hawking their services and touting their wares. The pungent smells of the quarter blended in the soft, warm air: soy sauce, boiling chickens, frying fat, garbage, urine.

Julia had done her Christmas shopping months ago, sending temple rubbings done by the students of the École des Beaux Arts and silver pepper mills and sugar bowls from the shops on "Silver Street" near the museum to friends and family in the States, but she wanted a small gift for Annie Fronton, who had invited her to a party in the teachers' quarters at the Lycée Descartes. The group would dine on dishes ordered from *La Taverne*, then walk the short distance to the city's neo-Gothic cathedral for Midnight Mass. Afterwards, they would return to Annie's for a traditional French Christmas Eve *réveillon* of champagne and *bûche de noël*.

As she got out of a *cyclo* in front of a small shop in the *quartier chinois* that sold *marrons glacés*, candied chestnuts imported from France, Julia caught a glimpse of Jake hurrying down the other side of the street, carrying some packages and walking fast, toward the waterfront.

That morning, Jake had received a package through the military mail system. Inside were two brightly wrapped Christmas presents, and a note from Nicole: She was very happy. She thanked Jake for all his acts of kindness. Chuck was to be discharged in January, and they planned to marry and go to the States. She missed the children and thought she would send for them later, when she and Chuck were settled.

The packages were toys, and she asked Jake to deliver them to her sister's home on Churi Changwar.

After he closed the consulate that evening, Jake walked through the *quartier chinois* toward the ferry that crossed to the island. In the quarter, people – Europeans mainly – were rushing around buying last-minute gifts. At the small, makeshift market near the ferry dock, Cambodians and Vietnamese who lived on the island were buying fried river fish from vendors with kerosene stoves, and the odor of frying fish and kerosene blended with the pungent sea-smell of the river. The ferry arrived, and the waiting crowd, many with bicycles heavily laden with bags of rice and charcoal and huge tins of cooking oil, moved down the long staircase to the boat, which was hot and dark and smelled of oil and was bathed in the amber glow of kerosene lamps. The small boat glided past junks and cargo ships and pleasure craft and reached the island after about ten minutes. *Cyclos* and horse-drawn carriages waited to take the passengers to their destinations, but Nicole had given Jake only vague directions, so he began to walk, asking people for the sister by name and getting only puzzled looks.

Soft winds from both the Mekong and Tonle Sap Rivers converged on the dark, tree-covered island and cooled the land so that Jake almost felt as if he were at home, walking along a country road. When he reached the Vietnamese quarter of the island, people were beginning to flock to the church for Christmas Eve Mass. The women were dressed in their best *hai-daos*, and the pastel, silk-like garments – blues, lavenders, and pinks – formed a half-festive, half-solemn procession along the moonlit river road.

The priest was standing on the church steps, greeting his parishioners, who parted like the Red Sea when Jake approached. He was French, and, yes, he knew Nicole and her sister. He stepped out into the lane and pointed to the house, a *paillote* like its neighbors, raised slightly off the ground and surrounded by a wooden fence with a cross over the gate.

Nicole's sister looked like her, only older. Nicole had written about the toys, and she had expected Jake, she said. She presented Nicole's children, a pretty little girl of about seven, who looked quite French, and a younger boy, darker and chubby. They shook hands shyly and muttered *"merci, monsieur""* for the gifts. The sister had four children of her own, and when they came in, he was sorry he hadn't brought more gifts.

Jake said goodnight and *Joyeux Noël* and promised to visit again. She smiled sadly, and they both knew he never would, and he walked back to catch the return ferry, which was practically empty. He stood on the deck alone and looked up at the stars.

When the boat landed, he walked home through the quiet streets and got very, very drunk.

Acquainted With Grief

From Julia's journal –Poor gallant Jake. He finally told me why he messed up on listening to Sihanouk's speech – taking Nicole to an abortionist. He says he plans to resign, marry his girl-back-home, and get a teaching job in rural Minnesota. Doomed to sackcloth and ashes on the Minnesota prairie because he threw away his career for a hard-as-nails bargirl who cheated on her boyfriend and abandoned her children.

Ambassador and Mrs. Braithwhite put out the word that they would be listening to Handel's *Messiah* on Christmas afternoon, and that the American community was welcome to join them. There was no Christmas tree, but a manger scene sat in the middle of the dining room table, and bowls of shiny Christmas balls festooned the bookshelves, brightening the sedate gathering. The sideboard was laden with sherry, Madeira, and fruitcake. Doris Braithwhite, the Ambassador's wife, poured tea at one end of the dining table, while her elderly mother, who lived with the couple, presided over the coffee urn at the other end. The guests – a scattering of Americans and other diplomats – listened to the music, talking only very quietly as the chorus and soloists retold the familiar story.

"He was despised and rejected of men," intoned the basso. "A man of sorrows and acquainted with grief."

A disheveled Sheila Grant entered the room, scanning the faces of the guests. She greeted the Braithwhites breathlessly, explaining she had returned early from a trip to the States, where her father was ill.

"Speaking of angels …" whispered Harper to Julia.

"I wanted to surprise Tom. I couldn't leave him alone on Christmas," Sheila said, again searching the room with her eyes. "Where is he?"

There was an awkward silence. Some of the guests knew that Tom Grant had taken advantage of his wife's absence to spend Christmas at a beachfront hotel in Penang with Elaine Murray.

"Sheila, Tom will be devastated," said Harper, stepping into the breach. "We needed an escort to go to Angkor with a visiting VIP, and since you and the kids weren't here, Tom volunteered."

She looked disappointed and rather annoyed but seemed to believe the lie. Then she plopped down on a sofa and looked as if she were going to settle in and enjoy the party. Harper didn't want that to happen, since the Ambassador was likely to start asking questions about the "visiting VIP" and give the ruse away.

"Sheila, you look beat," he said. "Let me take you home. Then I'll go to the Embassy and try to get word to Tom."

She started to protest, and, just then, Jake burst into the room. His eyes were bloodshot, and his speech was both loud and slurred.

"Merry Christmas, everybody," he shouted, waving a bottle of champagne at the Ambassador, who looked at it and Jake with disdain but mumbled a diplomatic "thank you."

"Come have some coffee, young man," said the Ambassador's mother, taking Jake by the elbow and leading him to the coffee urn.

While all eyes were on Jake, Harper took advantage of the situation to hustle Sheila out.

"Hallelujah!" he whispered to Julia as they left. "Thank God for a drunken vice-consul. Tom Grant would really be acquainted with grief if Sheila found out where he is."

Partir, C'est Mourir Un Peu

From Julia's journal—In a sense, so many of us here are "acquainted with grief." Jake with his career in ruins because of a bargirl. Tom and Elaine, whose love has no future. Peter with his faithless wife. Mary, whose husband left her with a baby and joined the underground with his mistress. Me, with my heart broken by Hourani. But where, for us, is the sound of trumpets, the crescendo of triumph, the Hallelujah Chorus? Most of us will simply muddle through, grab what happiness we can, and move on.

The morning Julia was to leave Phnom Penh for Saigon was the day Sihanouk had called a "National Congress of the Cambodian People" to rubber-stamp his decision to throw the Americans out.

"*Maman* says I must attend the *congrès*," Ket told her apologetically, excusing herself from seeing Julia off at the airport.

Julia nodded. She understood. Having worked for the hated Americans, Ket now needed to distance herself in order to survive.

Other Cambodian friends made similar excuses, and Julia had said goodbye to her American friends the night before – including Jake, whose drunken scene at the Ambassador's residence dealt the *coup de grace* to his Foreign Service career. He was packing up and would go home as soon as a replacement arrived.

That morning, she had only to take leave of Lanh and her family. Julia had found her a job with a French military family, but they wouldn't pay her as much and there were no quarters. She would have to leave the sunny room across from the kitchen she had been so happy to get. Julia gave her a month's wages and the bicycle she had bought but rarely used, and Lanh seemed almost pathetically grateful. There were tears in her eyes, but she squared her frail shoulders as if to say, "I am a refugee from North Viet Nam – a survivor."

Julia rode to Poochentong Airport with the Embassy driver, who was silent but obviously scared about his future. The normally sleepy little terminal bustled with activity, with departing Americans and people going to Hong Kong to celebrate the New Year, or even back to Paris.

Chantal, the young daughter of the murdered proprietor of the Bar Jean stood nervously in the Air France line, accompanied by a man from the bar. He asked an elderly French woman if she would look after the child, who would be met in Paris by relatives. The woman nodded, then turned to another elderly woman, possibly a sister, who was seeing her off.

"*Partir, c'est mourir un peu*," the old woman said. To leave is to die a little.

The Air Lao plane to Vientiane was called, and the family of the child who had been killed by the *cyclo* drivers started to board. The father had been transferred to Laos, and the wife carried a brass box that held the boy's ashes.

Mary, holding a squirming baby, came over to say goodbye. She still looked bewildered about Bo's desertion, not wanting to believe it, and she had obviously been crying. She would fly to Hong Kong, spend a night with friends there, and then head for Hawaii, where her parents would meet her.

In a corner of the waiting room, Julia glimpsed Hourani, with some people from his Embassy and Denise, who looked close to tears. So he was leaving on his long-talked-about world tour, she thought – oddly fitting for us to both be departing at the same time. He was waiting for the Djakarta plane. He would stop there enroute to Bali.

When his plane was called, Denise cried and clung to him, but he disengaged himself gently and climbed the stairway. At the top, he turned and blew a kiss, looking first toward her and then directly at Julia.

He smiled, and Julia, on impulse, clasped her hands together near her heart in a *namaste* and smiled back at him, knowing finally that she could say goodbye and leave this place but that Hourani – and all the joys and sorrows of her time here – would be hers forever.

Partir, c'est mourir un peu.

But, perhaps, as the Buddhists believe, to leave is to die a little and be reborn to live and love again, enriched and made wiser by the experience of the past.

Namaste.

Smiling through tears, she turned toward the Saigon plane.

Part 2: Endings – 1964 and beyond

Plaine des Jarres

From Julia's journal –
For Peter, Saigon, 1964

In the square beneath our window
Children dance a Pieter Brueghel scene.
Under the mosquito netting
I sip iced bouillon,
Listening for the sound of your key in the door.

The sound of the lock clicking open roused her from her reverie, and she parted the netting and rushed to the door to meet him.

"Hello, darling," he said in that deep, throaty voice with the faint trace of a New York accent – a voice that always made her body start to melt. He folded her in his arms, and she leaned against his chest, taking in the familiar smell of sweat and cigarette smoke and the perfumed soap the hotel laundry used on his shirts.

"How were the follies?" she asked, tilting her head back to look up at him.

"Same old crap," he said, his tender smile changing to a frown. "General Harkins insists the South Vietnamese army is making progress, but we all know they're losing ground. But let's talk about something else. In fact, let's not talk ..."

He pulled her back under the mosquito netting, and she started unbuttoning his shirt. They had developed a routine, "like old married people," he quipped. Julia would come to his room in the Continental after her workday at the Embassy and wait there while Peter attended the five o'clock press briefing at the headquarters of the US Military Assistance Group – dubbed by the correspondents, 'the five o'clock follies.' When he came back to the hotel, they would make love in the darkening room with its heavy mahogany furniture and mirrored armoire, then shower together in the cavernous, white-tiled bathroom and go somewhere for dinner. Afterwards, they'd return to the hotel and make love again, and, much later, Julia would return to the apartment the Embassy had found for her, on a quiet block near the Cercle Sportif Saigonnais.

When they emerged from the quiet darkness of the hotel lobby onto the noisy, sprawling terrace, the tables were filled with American military officers, foreign journalists and a few Vietnamese businesspeople enjoying pre-dinner drinks. A table of American reporters waved them over.

"We'll just say hello," Peter whispered. "There's a new UPI man who went on an operation down in the Delta today, and I want to hear how it went."

"Have you heard about the cable New York sent around to all the *Time* correspondents around the world?" asked the *Time* guy. "The phrase 'Let's have another one on Harry is in bad taste and should not be used.'"

They joined in the laughter but declined the offer to pull up chairs.

"We have a date with the new chef at Guillaume Tell," Peter told them. "Just wanted to welcome our new colleague…"

"Thanks," said the new man. "The welcome wagon greeted me at Long An this morning – it was a rout. The Vietnamese forces turned and ran, and the advisors and I barely made it to the helicopter in time."

"Baptism of fire," said Peter, his face darkening. He wanted the new government to be a successful prosecutor of the war, but he was clearly getting discouraged – the window of opportunity was closing.

They said their farewells and he took her arm and they crossed the noisy, bicycle-filled square and headed down Tu Do Street, which, in the days of French rule, had been Graham Greene's Rue Catinat. A light breeze ruffled the leaves of the tamarind trees that lined the street. The shops were still open, and Vietnamese women, looking like delicate flowers in their silky *hai-daos*, walked with linked arms, their high-pitched laughter echoing off the sidewalk like atonal music.

The popular restaurant was almost empty – it was early for dinner in Saigon – and they had their choice of seats. Peter chose a booth near the back, and they sat close together on the banquette and ordered *steak au poivre* and a bottle of Algerian red. When the waiter had poured the wine, Julia raised her glass and said, "*Santé.*"

"To us," Peter countered, looking into her eyes for a long moment and putting his hand over hers. "When we first met, I knew there was a spark between us, but I wasn't sure it would be fair to you to kindle it. It wasn't. I think I advised you to go home and settle down with your college sweetheart – and that's still good advice. But I've fallen in love with you, so I hope you don't take it. Are you willing to take a chance on a battle-scarred veteran of the marriage wars, darling? Not a very romantic proposal, I'm afraid."

"Yes, oh, yes…" was all she could say. Her throat was filled with a pressure that seemed to rise from the depths of her body, almost choking her, and her eyes filled with tears. He moved his hand under the table and squeezed her knee then rubbed her thigh and rested his hand between her legs until the waiter brought their steaks. He was hungry and ate his meal quickly, keeping the pressure on her thigh with his, but Julia could barely touch her steak and merely moved the *pommes frites* around her plate until he had finished his meal and paid the check. She wanted to go back to the room right away, but when they emerged from the restaurant on Tu Do, he guided her in the other direction, toward the Saigon River.

"Let's have a drink on the roof of the Majestic to celebrate," he said.

They climbed the stairs to the roof and took a small table, and he ordered a Scotch for himself and a *cognac-soda* for her. Dusk had turned to dark, but the sky was studded with stars, and in the distance, they could see orangey flashes on the ground.

"A fire fight around Bien Hoa," he told her. "The ARVN – the South Vietnamese forces – control the area in the daytime, at least nominally. But at night, the VC come out of the forest. I guess it's progress that the army is putting up a nighttime fight… I hope the fighting doesn't get any closer. Funny, when you're in love, you have hostages to fortune."

As they sipped their drinks, she moved her foot up and down the inside of his calf, and he soon felt her urgency. They hurried back to the hotel, arm in arm. That night, after the first quick, almost violent coupling, their lovemaking became slower, more tender and, afterward, they lay on their backs under the slow-moving ceiling fans and listened to the old songs Armed Forces Radio played late at night: *Poor Butterfly, Stars Fell on Alabama, This Is My First Affair* – songs Julia remembered her mother playing on the piano in the living room.

"This is my first affair – please, please be kind," he sang.

"You're not bad for a first timer," she joked.

"Smart ass," he said, and reached underneath her and grabbed her buttock and pulled her toward him.

The next afternoon, he had news.

"On both fronts," he laughed.

The divorce papers had come through, and his wife – now officially his ex-wife – was sending them to him to sign. And he had word from the government of Laos that its leader, Prince Souvanna Phouma, would grant him an interview next week.

"I'll take the Air Lao flight Monday morning," he said, and she could feel his excitement, feel him leaving her. It would always be like that, she knew. She would never possess him completely.

"The one I really want to talk with is Souvanaphuong, the Communist Prince, but I'll work on that when I get to Vientiane. Not sure how the connections are to Luang Prabang, so I may be away a week or so," he added. "But it will be wonderful knowing I have you to come home to. *Home*. I like the sound of that."

When he had been gone for more than a week, she began to worry. He had kept his room at the Continental, but they told her at the desk they hadn't seen him. Then she went around to the five o'clock briefing to see if any of his colleagues had heard anything.

She stood at the back of the crowded room. The briefing officer, a young major, took the podium with a somber air.

"This afternoon, I have very bad news," he began. "Your colleague, Peter Stein, was a passenger in an Air America plane that crashed this morning on the Plain of Jars, shortly after taking off from Luang Prabang. There were no survivors. We have all lost a friend, and a perceptive and careful journalist."

There was a collective gasp, and the briefing officer shuffled some papers, cleared his throat, and continued.

"Yesterday ARVN forces bested Viet Cong guerillas near the strategic hamlet of Tan Hiep..."

Julia's body went limp. She had to hold onto the wall to keep from falling. She slipped out of the room and walked through the streets in a trance. Once inside her apartment, she finally let herself cry.

She went through the next few months in a sort of mechanical daze – grinding out upbeat press releases about the progress of the war, trying to place stories about American culture in a profoundly uninterested press, swimming laps at the Cercle Sportif, putting in appearances at Embassy events. When President Johnson committed American troops to fight beside the ARVN forces, the call went out for Embassy officers to work in the provinces, directly aiding the war effort. She quickly volunteered. She had nothing to lose, and maybe it would bring her closer to Peter, somehow. But they turned her down, as she knew they would. A war zone was no place for a woman, they said, and she knew she would soon be transferred to another, more peaceful post.

Tired of it all, she remembered Peter's advice to "go home and marry your college sweetheart – but not yet."

Perhaps she would do that – perhaps it was time.

The Color of the Sea Queen

From Julia's journal – At times, the people I knew in Phnom Penh seem more real to me than the ones I see every day. But never mind – I'm happy enough. I wonder about Elaine, though. I doubt she's with Tom, but I hope she, too, has landed on her feet – that she's not still teaching English in some third-world backwater...

Elaine Murray eased her car – a brand-new Austin-Healy Sprite convertible with red leather seats –out of the suburb-like enclave of Kebajaran into the squalid streets of Djatinegara. She drove as fast as she dared, embarrassed by the poorly dressed people who stood outside their tin-roofed shanties, staring. Squat banana palms sat in trash-strewn yards. Tea stalls and vendors of *saté* – roasted chicken or fish on skewers – and clove-stuffed cigarettes, called *kreteks*, encroached on the already overcrowded road. *Ganjang Malaysia* was scrawled on every available surface.

"What does that mean?" asked her passenger, Richard Becker, a visiting law professor.

"Crush Malaysia," she explained, somewhat surprised that he didn't seem to know about *konfrontasi*, Indonesia's running feud with its prosperous neighbor to the north. She drove on in silence, still smarting at the fact that her friend, Dan, who had organized the seaside picnic, had saddled her with Becker.

I guess Dan meant to do me a favor, she thought bitterly. *An eligible man.*

Cars, mini-buses, scooters, and bicycles clogged the road – people thronging to get out of Djakarta on a Sunday – and horns blared. Chickens skittered back and forth, dodging cars.

"Tell me about yourself," Becker requested, sounding professorial.

"Not much to tell," she replied. "I'm 31, born in Chicago, majored in English at University of Illinois–"

"I didn't mean a resume," he laughed. "I can see by your left hand that you're not married. Attached? Really none of my business–"

"You're right," she snapped. "It's none of your business."

Was she attached? Even she didn't know the answer. Before she had received Tom's letter, she would have said yes, definitely yes. But now...

Becker seemed to lose interest in her love life as the scenery improved. As they climbed toward Bogor, the landscape became greener, lusher, and the houses less tawdry. Red tile roofs replaced the ubiquitous metal, and white-painted bamboo formed picket fences along the road.

"Bogor – my God – the famous botanical garden is here," Becker exclaimed suddenly, jolting Elaine from her reverie. "Can we stop?"

Elaine looked pointedly at her watch. Their destination, Pelabuhanratu, on the Indian Ocean coast, was only 90 miles from Djakarta, but the route was mountainous, and the roads were pot-holed and clogged with traffic. They still had two or more hours to go, and the salad she had brought was probably wilting in the cooler in the trunk.

"Please," he said, sensing her hesitation and putting a hand on hers. "Just for a few minutes."

She nodded and pulled the car into the already crowded parking lot. They took a map from the kiosk and set out along a path.

"What do you want to see exactly?" she queried impatiently.

Kebun Raya, the Indonesian name for the gardens, was vast. If they browsed the entire sprawling complex, they'd be here for hours.

"I adore orchids," he said, looking at the map. "But they're indoors, and it's too nice to go inside...Oh, here, this is what we simply must see, the *Amorphophallus*. I don't think I need translate. Come on, let's go see this infamous phallic symbol."

"All right," she said, ignoring his snide look. "Though you may lose your appetite for the picnic."

A small crowd had gathered around the flower, whose conical three-foot long center jutted obscenely upwards from its broad purplish petals. One young Indonesian couple in the front row held hands – the man giggling, the woman blushing shyly. But no one got too close to the flower – its odor was overwhelming, like rotting meat. Children held their noses, backing away.

"It's sometimes called 'the corpse flower,'" said the guide. "The smell is thought to attract the insects needed to pollinate the flower. Actually, despite this strong attraction, pollination can be difficult. That is because the flowers lie deep inside at the base of the *spadix*, the conical structure. And the female flowers develop before the male flowers are ready."

"Ah, would-be lovers at cross purposes," Becker said in an undertone.

"We're lucky. We got here at the right time. Its bloom is short-lived. It will soon deflate," Elaine whispered, suppressing a smile.

Becker laughed: "*Sic transit gloria…*" and they headed toward the car. At least he had a sense of humor. Maybe he wasn't such a pompous ass after all.

"Elaine, lovely lady, would you do me the honor of letting me drive your wonderful car?" he pleaded.

She started to refuse, but she was tired, and maybe if he drove she could take a quick nap before they arrived. Or just think. She had some decisions to make.

"All right," she agreed, and tossed him the keys.

After Bogor, the road climbed past terraced rice fields and tea plantations on the slopes of Gunung Salak, whose peak was shrouded by puffy cumulus clouds.

"Tell me about yourself," she asked. "Though it's none of my business, of course."

"I'm an open book," he said good-naturedly. "I'm 44, heterosexual, married once, divorced once, gainfully employed as a professor at Georgetown Law School—"

"And you were a classmate of Dan's at Yale," she interrupted.

"Yes – great guy, Dan," he replied. "Always very reticent, circumspect. I take it Wiratmo is a love interest?"

Wiratmo, a lanky young Javanese who taught at the University of Indonesia Faculty of Law and was Becker's host at the law school, was in Dan's car, along with his mother. A third car held a young Indonesian woman named Aurora and her boyfriend, a Dutch archeologist named Van Hoek.

Elaine shrugged. She didn't want to talk about Dan's personal life. Any intimations of homosexuality would doom his Foreign Service career.

"Again, none of my business," he said.

The road began to descend to the coastal plain. A herd of water buffalo trotted ahead, slowing traffic. After the blaring of many horns, the farmer led the animals into a field, and the flow of cars resumed.

"There's a village up ahead. You'd better slow down," warned Elaine.

In rural Java, people lived much of their lives on the roads, ignoring traffic. Here, the villagers were walking on both sides of the narrow road, pushing carts, pulling wagons.

"Look, a rather large mosque for such a small town," said Becker, ignoring her caution and pointing to a whitewashed dome with a metal crescent at its pinnacle.

It was right then that she heard it – a distinct thud, then a cry.

"Stop!" she ordered.

Becker had swerved slightly as he looked at the mosque, hitting a young boy.

"Oh my god," he said. "I've hit someone. Change places with me – I don't have an Indonesian drivers' license..."

She was furious and a little scared. Perhaps it made sense. She did have a local driver's license. But she was a teacher. She didn't have diplomatic immunity. What sort of trouble would she be in? And what kind of a man would let her take the blame for something like this? Not a man like Tom, with his well-developed sense of honor. Honor, how she had hated the word when he used it in connection with his marriage. *I could not love thee, dear so much, loved I not honor more*. But now—

She got out of the car to look at the child. He was clutching his leg and crying but didn't seem to be seriously hurt. Thank God. Richard stood by the car as if in a trance, trembling and looking stricken. She pushed him into the passenger seat, where he sat with his head in his hands.

A crowd was beginning to gather. They had warned about this in the Embassy orientation session. *Amok*, the administrative officer had explained, was a Malay-Indonesian word. She wished they had not lagged so far behind the others. Wiratmo could have spoken to the villagers in Javanese – or was it Sundanese they were speaking? Elaine had picked up some rudimentary *Bahasa Indonesia*, but spoke it only haltingly and, in the villages, the regional languages were more likely to be spoken.

The crowd was pressing closer to the car now, and the volume getting louder. Suddenly, the noise quieted, and the people clustered around the driver's side of the car stepped back. A tall European in the brown robe of a monk approached. He knelt on the ground and spoke to the boy, then got up and addressed Elaine.

"He will be all right," the monk said in accented English. He must be Dutch, she guessed.

"Oh, thank God," she said. "I mean, I'm sorry…"

"It's all right," he smiled, showing large, crooked teeth. "It is quite proper to thank God. The boy will go to his village headman, who will give him an *obat* –a folk remedy, but they believe in such things."

"But perhaps we should take him to a hospital," she said. "I think there's one in Bogor…"

"Oh, no," said the priest. "He would never go. He has probably never left the village. He would be afraid."

The villagers stood back a little, watching the priest. He looked down at the ground, shuffling his feet, which were clad in sandals. His yellowing toenails were covered with dirt from the road.

"But perhaps a gift to the village headman would be in order," he said, embarrassed.

"Of course," she said, and elbowed Richard, who pulled out his wallet, as if in a trance.

"I have only dollars," he said feebly.

Elaine opened her purse.

"How much would be appropriate, Father?" she asked.

"Oh, five thousand *rupiahs* would be very generous…"

She quickly pulled out ten thousand, a pittance by the Embassy's favorable exchange rate.

"And maybe I could make a small gift to your church?" she asked.

"As you wish," he said, and she put another ten thousand *rupiah* note in his large, callused hand.

The priest spoke to the crowd, which dispersed quickly, people returning to their normal routines as if they had been released from a freeze-frame.

She drove slowly out of the village, looking straight ahead.

"I wonder if they pull that trick often," said Becker, suddenly perking up.

"I guess the priest is in on it," he added cynically, turning his head slightly to see her reaction.

She looked at him, repelled, then turned her eyes back to the road and drove on silently.

The country flattened out. Rice paddies stretched down to the sea, which was visible in the distance, a faint turquoise line. She thought of the times she and Tom had spent together by the sea. That one night in Kep, that stolen Christmas in Penang, their last meeting in Bali. Those were, she supposed, the "moment of the rose" that Tom had promised would be theirs forever.

"These precious moments," he had written, "will sustain me through a lifetime of loneliness, and the tedium of the Foreign Service will be bearable to me, knowing that I experienced a great love. When Sheila and I met at Cornell, she was a sorority girl. I was a dairy farmer's son on a scholarship. I was a bit in awe of her, and when she dropped out of college to marry me, I was so grateful. I didn't know real love until ours. But, my dearest, I can't, with honor, leave Sheila. And I can't, with honor, keep you from finding a measure of happiness. You're still young – you'll meet someone else…"

Someone like Becker? she wondered.

They were approaching the town of Pelabuhanratu – just a jumble of shanties and stalls. Following Wiratmo's directions, she turned right at the marketplace, edging closer to the sea. For a fleeting moment, she imagined herself here with Tom. Unlike Becker, he would have taken care of her. He would have acted with courage and honor. Would she always hold Tom up as a standard? Would no one else ever measure up?

Honor, she thought bitterly. Was that what was keeping them apart. A small voice within her wondered if Tom's reasons for the breakup were totally unselfish, totally honorable. He was rising in the Foreign Service. He made no secret of his ambition to be an Ambassador someday. A scandal, a mistress – how she hated that word – would dim his prospects.

They were at the seafront now. A thick row of casuarina pines separated the road from a long black sand beach.

"There they are," said Becker, shouting like an excited child on an outing.

The group was gathered under the pines around a large batik tablecloth. Ibu, Wiratmo's mother, sat in a folding chair, chatting in Dutch – her preferred language – with Van Hoek while the others lounged on pillows. Everyone waved, and Dan and Wiratmo and Van Hoek came over to the car.

"We were worried," said Dan. "Did you have an accident?"

Becker was silent, and Elaine hesitated for only a moment.

"We stopped in Bogor," she said. "At the botanical garden."

"Ah, the *Kebun Raya*," said Van Hoek, approvingly. "Are the vanilla orchids in bloom?"

"I wanted to see them," said Becker, slowly coming to life. "But Elaine insisted on taking me to see the famous phallic flower."

Slamming down the trunk, Elaine handed the now wilted salad to Dan.

Dan probably thinks he made a pass – or that I did, she thought, seething but relieved by their tacit agreement not to talk about the accident with the child.

"Are you okay?" Dan whispered, taking the salad bowl.

"Fine," she said, forcing a smile. "Just tired, hot – and hungry."

Wiratmo had bought cold lobsters at the fish market in the small town, and Van Hoek had brought champagne in a cooler. Elaine sank down on the sand, which was blessedly cool. She only half-listened to the conversation, concentrating instead on the rhythmic crash of the breakers on the nearby shore.

Aurora seemed to be staring at her oddly, and, catching her reflection in the metal champagne bucket, Elaine saw that her long, dark hair must had been blown to a frenzy- making her look like a mad woman, a Medusa.

"I'm famished," said Elaine, grabbing a lobster and attacking it with unladylike ferocity.

She dipped the cold, succulent meat in the chili-laced mayonnaise that Dan had brought and washed it down with champagne. She could feel her face getting redder, either from the alcohol or hot peppers, and even the sliced mangoes that Aurora offered for dessert failed to cool her off.

Elaine stood up. "I have to swim," she said, looking at the ocean.

"Too rough today," advised Ibu. "People have drowned here."

Her father had taught her to swim on the Lake Michigan beaches, and she was never afraid of the sea. She found it to be, instead, a kindred spirit.

"I'll be all right," she assured them.

Champagne courage, perhaps.

She should have gone behind a bush to change, but she was suddenly in a hurry and she had worn a bathing suit under her clothes. Stepping back a few feet from the picnic cloth, she pulled her shirt over her head and unzipped her linen slacks.

"Your bathing suit, Elaine," stammered Aurora. "It's green."

Tom had liked her in green. He said it brought out her green eyes, her Black Irish beauty. She had bought the bathing suit just before their Christmas together – their only Christmas together— in Penang. He said it made her look like a mermaid, she remembered.

"Green is the color of *Nyai Loro Kidul*," Wiratmo explained, looking embarrassed. "The *Ratu Kidul* – the queen of the southern sea. She controls the waves, and if you take her color, she will be jealous and take you – take your life."

She stared at him in disbelief. He was an educated person, a professor.

"Superstition, to be sure," said Van Hoek, sensing her reaction. "But why tempt fate?"

She folded her clothes and walked out of the casuarinas to the sea's edge, which was fringed with palms. Dan followed.

"Elaine," he said diffidently. "It *is* unusually rough today, and there are no lifeguards…"

"Oh, Dan," she interrupted. "Don't you know by now there are never really any lifeguards, that, in the end, we're all on our own? Here, hold my sunglasses, please."

She walked quickly into the waves. The water, though warm as the Indian Ocean always was, felt cool on her overheated body. Finding a window of opportunity, she quickly dove under a wave, which rolled over her with a great force. When it had passed, she jumped up quickly and waved back to the nervous group that had gathered on the beach. Take that, sea queen, she thought triumphantly, then dove under just in time to escape another pounding wave. They were coming quickly, and she felt herself tiring. But it felt good to have no adversary but the ocean, no goal other than to survive, and Elaine was a survivor…

Green, the color of the sea. The color of hope in Catholic liturgy. The color of peace in Islam. But, mainly, the color of jealousy. Elaine knew a thing or two about that green-eyed monster. Oh, yes, she could go toe-to-toe with the *Ratu Kidul* on jealousy …

A huge wave knocked her out of her reverie, and she rode it into the beach. Dan stood there with a towel he had retrieved from her car, and she wrapped herself in it. She was exhausted, gasping, spent, but it felt good to have bested the sea queen.

When they rejoined the group, the other women were already packing up the picnic things.

"If you don't mind, I'm going to ride back with Van Hoek," said Becker. "We want to compare notes on orchids."

She nodded coldly and said her goodbyes to the others, relieved to be able to drive back alone with her thoughts.

The next weekend, the Bulgarian Ambassador drowned at Pelabuhanratu. The newspapers didn't mention the color of his bathing suit. Elaine wondered whether it had been green or whether the vengeance of the sea queen had simply been delayed.

*****

She had come 'First Class/Non-Air Conditioned,' which was how the upper-class Indians traveled and was exponentially cheaper than "First Class/Air Conditioned." But, despite the genteel trappings of faded luxury, her compartment had been hot and dusty, and the overnight train journey from Calcutta to Puri had been tiring.

Elaine Murray had lived in Calcutta almost five years, teaching English in a high school for girls and living at Russell's Hotel, a charming though somewhat seedy hostelry on a leafy street in the once elegant, now shabby-genteel Garden District, run by a genial Armenian. She had made a few friends in the ex-pat community and among the Indian teachers at the school, but most weekends and vacations she spent traveling by herself, and India's innumerable temples with their frequent festivals were the most obvious destination. Most, she had found disappointing.

Her first foray had been an arduous bus trip to Khajuraho – a journey that involved an overnight in a very spare, none-too-clean government bungalow – to see the famous erotic sculptures, which, if truth be told, she found more grotesque than erotic. She had gone all the way to Madras for the Holi Festival, which involved a lot of boisterous spray-painting and a huge bonfire to burn Kama, the God of Love, in effigy. The fireworks at the Deepavali Festival made her think of those she and Tom had watched long ago soaring and descending over Angkor Wat. At the Ganesh Festival in Bombay, she had unwisely bought *modaks*, the traditional coconut dumplings, from a street vendor and got so sick she had to spend most of the festival in her hotel room. It was

171

a silly holiday anyway, she decided, dedicated to an elephant god with only one tusk because he had thrown the other at the moon. How futile, she thought, how Indian! But she had high hopes for the Rath Yatra, the celebration of the Jagganath, the lord of the universe, the juggernaut or irresistible force that crushes everything in its path. She wanted something elemental from India, something she couldn't define or describe. Not spirituality, exactly… maybe a sort of finality.

First, however, she wanted a swim, to wash away the heat and the dust and the fatigue. From the balcony of her room in the old wooden pile that was the Great Southern Railway Hotel, she gazed down at the wide, almost deserted beach and the boardwalk that led to the Bay of Bengal. It was only a few weeks before the monsoon, and the sea was sultry, dark and threatening under an overcast sky. She quickly changed into her suit, the green maillot she had worn the Christmas she and Tom had spent in that wonderful beach hotel in Penang. It still fit, she thought with satisfaction as she gazed at herself in the full-length mirror.

Not bad for 39, she decided. She was, if anything, thinner than in her younger days, and her stomach was flat, and her small breasts didn't sag. Still, next year she would turn 40, and she had found a few gray hairs – harbingers of things to come. In the teacher's lounge, she had overheard one of her colleagues say to another: "Miss Murray never married."

Never.

At first, she was stung by the finality of the word, which consigned her to eternal spinsterhood. Then she remembered that most Indian women were married off by the parents as teenagers and were grandmothers by the time they reached her age and shrugged it off. There had been several men in her life after Tom, but none had measured up.

She threw a terry cloth robe over her suit and went downstairs. As she stepped down from the hotel porch, she was suddenly surrounded by a dozen dark, sinewy Bengali men in abbreviated bathing suits and rubber caps, who formed a gauntlet along the boardwalk leading to the sea.

"Madame, Madame," they all called out at once, reaching for her hand.

At first, she didn't understand what they wanted. They were too able-bodied for beggars. Then she saw a young Indian man, pale and probably from the north, walking timidly into the water with one of the Bengalis holding tight to his arm.

They were lifeguards. One-on-one lifeguards. For a few rupees, they would attach themselves to you and save you if need be. But who could enjoy a swim with someone hanging on your arm? It would obviate the whole purpose of swimming in the Sea—the glorious, elemental freedom of it. A strong swimmer, Elaine loved the sea, even – or especially – in its rawest state. Disdaining the services of the guards, she shed her terry cloth robe, squared her shoulders and walked quickly into the water, ignoring their shrill calls.

After all, she thought, laughing to herself, in Indonesia she had defied the notorious queen of the south sea by swimming there in this same green bathing suit – despite warnings that the goddess reserved that color for herself and would kill anyone who usurped it. And the sea there was much more formidable than the Bay of Bengal.

She walked out a little then dove under a wave. The dark clouds hung low, turning the sea a dull gray, but the water, though tepid, was colder than the air, and instantly made her feel more alive. She swam out about thirty feet, then turned to face the shore. She floated on her back for a minute and felt the current pulling her strongly, to the right and slightly out to sea. On the shore – which seemed more distant than it should have –the guards were watching her with somewhat sinister interest. Then she felt a swell beneath the surface and realized she had drifted out farther than she thought. She quickly headed back to shore, fighting the undertow with a strong crawl, and riding the last ten feet into shore on a breaking wave, landing hard on the sand at the water's edge. More tired than she wanted to admit, she pushed herself up and walked back on the boardwalk through the gauntlet of the smirking guards.

Back in her room, she pulled the curtains shut and lay down on her bed and fell immediately asleep. She had slept little on the train the night before, and the workout in the sea, far from purging her body of fatigue, had exhausted it. She woke up a few hours later bathed in sweat. The closed curtains had cut off any possibility of a breeze, and the ceiling fan simply blew the hot air around. She showered, then dressed quickly and headed to the temple complex.

Had she known in advance that non-Hindus were prohibited from Jagganath Temple, she might not have come. A high wall surrounded the vast, sprawling temple complex, and all she could see were the peak-like towers of the ornate sandstone temples. Guards – as well as two imposing stone lions – presided over the gate. She had to be content with watching the preparations to tomorrow's procession from the roof of the Raghunandan Library. Non-Hindus were impure, she supposed, gazing over the temple wall at the wedding-cake-like towers, which looked like the castles she had made of wet sand on the shores of Lake Michigan when she was a child.

The Rath Yatra was also called the "car festival." When she first heard the term, she thought it referred to something like the *Concours d'Elégance* she had participated in back in Cambodia. A car dealer in Phnom Penh, whose son she taught at the *lycée*, asked her to drive a Chevy Impala in this silly imitation of a French custom. An American girl for an American car. She agreed only because it involved a weekend in Kep, a beach resort on the Gulf of Siam. Somehow, Tom managed to come, too and although they had separate rooms, they had been able to spend a whole night together, for the first time. Almost the only time. It had been wonderful falling asleep in his arms after making love, and waking up in the early light and finding him beside her and making love again… she supposed he must be an Ambassador by now. That was why he wouldn't leave Sheila, no matter what he said about honor, she thought with a touch of bitterness.

But this "car festival" – really a chariot festival – was different, less frivolous, somehow – at least she hoped so.

The chariots were huge wooden structures mounted on at least a dozen heavy wheels. The largest held a giant statue of Lord Jagganath, one of the manifestations of Krishna. Built to look like the Jagganath Temple itself, it towered almost fifty feet and was festooned with jewel-encrusted tents and had a platform large enough to hold a retinue of dignitaries and priests. Two slightly smaller vehicles carried images, or *murtis*, of Krishna's brother and sister.

This afternoon, devotees were putting the finishing touches on the chariots, attaching brightly colored flags and festooning the vehicles with flowers. She watched until it got dark, then walked back to the hotel and ate an early, solitary dinner in the cavernous dining room. The chariot procession would take place the next morning, and she wanted to get to the library early to get a good view.

The noise of the crowd was deafening as Elaine climbed the steps that led to the library roof. The local tourist bureau had provided an English-speaking guide to narrate the events for the non-Hindus, though there were only a few – a Muslim family from the Punjab and a middle-aged German couple.

"Ladies and gentlemen," the guide began, "you are about to witness the sacred journey, or *yatra*, of Lord Jagganath and his brother, Baladhardra and his sister Subhadra from their home in the main temple to the Gundicha Temple. Symbolically, this is a journey from light to darkness…"

Light to darkness, she thought. Life to death. Being to nothingness. Maybe that was what Nirvana was all about.

"Listen – you hear the gongs?" he said excitedly. "That is the signal that the deities are boarding the vehicles."

Ear-splitting booms momentarily drowned out the roar of the crowd, and devotees – like pallbearers – lifted the statues to their perches in the chariots.

"The god with the yellow face – that is Subhadra," said the guide, fully into the excitement of the moment. "And Baladhardra has a white face."

At a signal from an official mounted on a horse, the procession began, with Baladardra's chariot in the lead, pulled by a horde of devotees, young boys mainly, screaming with excitement.

"It is not true that the devotees are fanatics who throw themselves under the wheels to achieve martyrdom," said the guide, rather indignantly. "That unfortunate rumor was started by Christian missionaries with the purpose of discrediting the Hindu religion. But, sometimes, of course, there are accidents… Sometimes the followers get too close – and the Jagganath is going so fast it can't be stopped."

A tumultuous cheer rose from the crowd when Lord Jagganath's chariot, its platform crowded with dignitaries, joined the procession. Hordes of costumed Hindus followed, some on foot, some on horseback, and the people who lined the road threw flowers, even little cakes. Elaine craned her neck to follow the chariot with her eyes until it finally disappeared in a cloud of brown dust.

"The deities will go to Gundicha Temple, where they will rest for eight days," continued the guide. "On the ninth day, they will be returned to the Jagganath Temple here. I hope you will come back at the time to welcome the deities home… Meanwhile, I hope you have enjoyed this talk. I am a government-licensed guide…"

He placed a small basket on a stool near the staircase, for tips, of course, and Elaine placed a few rupees in it before descending the stairs. The streets, cleared of many of the devotees, who were following the procession, were almost quiet, but the dust the crowds had churned up was overwhelming. She cut over to a side road, hoping she could still find the way back to the hotel.

Colorful as it was, the procession had been a disappointment. Rather than an elemental, irresistible force, the Jagganath's chariot had seemed more like something out of a Halloween parade. And instead of going from light to darkness, it had simply journeyed to another festival down the road. She felt strangely let down, but the thought of a swim to wash away the dust revived her, and she quickened her pace.

Back at the hotel, she hurried to change, and when she got to the beach, the sky was already darkening, and the sea was churning harder than she had observed it before. The guards eyed her with little interest, resigned to the fact that she would not hire them. She practically ran across the beach to the water, then slowed as the waves seemed to push her back.

Just a quick swim, she thought, her energy flagging, but there was little time for thought. She dove under a large incoming wave and felt the force above her knock her head down against the sand. When she rose to the surface, she found herself turned in the direction of the beach, where the guards were clustered in a knot, watching her intently, their arms folded across their chests. She smiled at them as another wave caught her, pulling her under and away from the shore. She fought it for a few minutes, then decided it was probably a rip tide and you were not supposed to resist it but to swim with it. Relieved, she let it carry her out and, soon, the shore began to recede, then disappeared.

"Tom," she called, and for a fleeting moment, she saw him, standing on the beach at Penang that long-ago Christmas, waving to her. But it was only the guards, staring impassively out to sea.

Suddenly, a huge wave hit her from the side.

The juggernaut, the irresistible force, she whispered to herself as she went under for the final time and completed the journey from light to darkness.

Miss Murray never married, and there were no immediate survivors. She had, however, achieved a kind of immortality – in the stories the guards would tell for many years to any potential customers who dared to resist their offers of service.

The Dead Heart of Africa

From Julia's journal – Note from Bill Harper on their Christmas card: Tom Grant was named Ambassador to Chad. Sheila must be making life hell for the other officers' wives...

The dry season in the south of the country began in October, and hot desert air from the north descended on the capital, which was named Fort Lamy for a dead French soldier – killed in a battle just across the Chari River. The country was Chad, often called "The Dead Heart of Africa" for its landlocked status and for the fact that except for a small belt between the capital and the marshlands of Lake Chad, it was a desert.

Appropriate that he should be Ambassador here, thought Tom Grant as he sat in a café on the quay and sipped a Pernod and watched the sun set over the river. One dead heart deserves another.

When he was nominated for the ambassadorship, he was thrilled. Even though it was Chad, it was some sort of recognition of his worth, a reward for a lifetime of slogging in the trenches of the third world. He thought Sheila would be pleased, but her face fell when he told her. She had long since given up pipe dreams of being posted in London or Paris, but she'd hoped for a Washington tour. And Fort Lamy with its poverty, squalor, and hot climate was just one more cross for her to bear.

He thought she might at least enjoy being the Ambassador's wife, even in a small pond. But the Foreign Service had changed, and the other Embassy wives were no longer expected to kowtow. None of them had the time or inclination, anyway. His deputy's wife, a French anthropologist, spent most of her time in the field. The Public Affairs Officer's wife drank and, reportedly, slept around, though he was no longer allowed to mention such peccadilloes in the officer's fitness report. Not that he would have – Jack was a nice old guy desperately counting the years to his pension. The Economic Officer was a single woman who had, quite correctly, resisted Sheila's attempt to treat her as an embassy wife. The Admin officer's wife, an accountant, worked full time running the Budget and Fiscal Office. Sheila might have made friends among the small diplomatic community, but she had never learned French, their common language.

The sun disappeared behind the low mud-brick buildings across the river in Kousséri, in Cameroon, and Tom laid some money on the table. Here, so close to the equator, sunsets didn't linger, and Sheila was expecting him. He had suggested they go out to dinner for her last night in Fort Lamy. The French hadn't done much good in their six decades here, but they had left some good restaurants. But she had refused, as he knew she would. When they first arrived, Sheila had gotten sick after a dinner at *La Parisienne*, the best in town, and since then, had never trusted Fort Lamy's restaurants. Instead, they ate at home —mainly canned goods from the small Embassy commissary, local produce that had had the life soaked out of it in lye, and frozen meat flown in from South Africa.

He left the café and walked across the dark, unpaved street to where his driver, Abou, was waiting, dozing over the steering wheel.

"Chez moi, Abou, s'il vous plaît," he said, probably unnecessarily since he rarely went anyplace else but home. When he first came, he used to get a big kick out of riding in his official car with the small US flags flying from it, but the novelty quickly wore off. There were few paved roads and few places of real interest. Most of the country was desert. And, just as the dry desert winds were descending on the capital from the north, so were the winds of change. Slowly but inexorably,

Islamic insurgents from the north were advancing on Fort Lamy. Soon, the capital and its US-supported dictator would be under siege to the rebels, just as they were to the creeping Sahara. At least, that was what Tom kept saying in reports back to Washington – reports, he suspected, that were read with little interest – if they were read at all. The story of his career.

The residence was a fine old colonial house with a lawn that probably required enough water to supply a small desert village, Tom reflected as he stepped out of the car under the portico. At home, they'd never have been able to afford such a house. Not to mention servants.

"*Madame est en haut – elle fait les valises,*" Fatima, the maid, told him.

Sheila was upstairs, packing.

It sometimes seemed she had been packing and unpacking their whole married life. They had started dating his senior year at Cornell. He had been an English major, with vague aspirations to be a writer – much to the chagrin of his dairy-farmer father who wanted him in the Ag school. Then Sheila got pregnant, and a friend told him about the Foreign Service exam, which was given on campus. He passed, and Sheila was elated – she had never been to Europe, she'd said excitedly. But after the training program in Washington – where Tom,

Jr. was born – he was assigned to Vientiane. Sheila hadn't minded it too much. They were young, and still in love, and there were trips to Bangkok, even Hong Kong. Then came Kuala Lumpur and Manila, where their daughter, Susan, was born. By that time, Sheila was sick of smelly, dirty cities in hot, humid countries whose food always made her sick, she said. And then they were transferred to Phnom Penh, where he met Elaine.

He should go up and help her pack or at least say hello, but he asked Idris, the houseboy, to bring a gin-tonic to the verandah, and sat out there in one of the rattan chairs. Sheila stayed mainly in the air-conditioned bedroom in the evenings and shunned the verandah, which was not screened against insects. But he loved to sit there and watch the African night close in around him and listen to the chirping of the gecko lizards.

"*A l'heure quand le gecko gemit.*"

That had been the phrase he and Elaine used to fix their clandestine meetings – at the hour when the gecko chirps. Five o'clock in her apartment near the river. Shabby, run-down – and paradise. After a magical hour or two with Elaine – a *cinq à sept*, as the French called such trysts, he could go home and listen to Sheila's litany of complaints with equanimity. He and Elaine fell hopelessly in love, but there was nothing he could do about it. He finally broke it off. He told himself it was for Elaine's sake. She was young and could meet someone else. But, to be honest, he was also thinking about his career. Divorce, commonplace now in the Foreign Service, was frowned upon then, and scandals were grounds for dismissal. So, he had lost Elaine and, in due time, gained an ambassadorship. Ambassador to the dead heart of Africa. He suddenly remembered the question framed on the wall of his long-ago Sunday-school classroom. "What does it profit a man to gain the whole world and suffer the loss of his soul?"

Or his heart.

Sheila's high heels clicked down the marble staircase, and he rose to go inside and greet her.

"Good evening, Tom," she said, somewhat formally.

"Sheila, dear, you look nice," he responded.

She had put on a sundress for the occasion, one she probably wouldn't be taking back to Washington, where fall was well underway. But her face was red and blotchy – she had obviously been crying. Not over her departure from him or from Fort Lamy, he knew. In other circumstances, she would have been thrilled to go home. But she had found a lump in her left breast, and a biopsy showed it was malignant. The Embassy doctor thought some lymph nodes might be involved, which would be very bad news, but he wasn't certain, and Sheila needed to go home immediately for state-of-the-art diagnostics and treatment. She would be treated at Bethesda. Surgery, then possibly chemotherapy or radiation or both. A grim prospect, an unknown outcome.

At dinner, they spoke mainly of the children and of the complicated logistics of her move. Tommy was at Cornell, and Susan at Deerfield Academy, and Sheila would see them soon. No need for them to come out at Christmas, as they had planned. Instead, Tom would go to the States. They had managed to get the tenants out of their home in Arlington, and he was trying to arrange to get their furniture out of storage.

She repeated all the instructions about the servants that they had gone over before. How much each got paid and how much to give the cook for shopping.

"You'll probably eat out most of the time when I'm gone, so you can cut that in half," Sheila said.

She had an early plane next morning, to Dakar and Paris, where she would switch to an American carrier. The driver was waiting, and the suitcases loaded in the car, as they downed a silent, hurried breakfast. Nor did they speak as they drove the few miles through the quiet streets to the small airport on the edge of the city.

Because he had diplomatic plates, they were allowed to drive right out onto the tarmac. Abou paid his respects to Sheila, which she acknowledged with a nod, then he went off to have a cigarette and give them some privacy.

"Just think – you're taking off from the same airport as Amelia Earhart," he said, just to make conversation. The doomed aviator had stopped briefly in Fort Lamy in 1937. Remembering Earhart's fate, he instantly regretted the remark.

"If I die, you'll be free to marry her ... the teacher ... Elaine," she burst out. She had never spoken the name to him before.

"You thought I didn't know? I'm not that stupid," she said, her voice breaking and her eyes filling with tears.

This was this cue to take her in his arms, to comfort her, to tell her he had always loved her, but he just stared out the window.

The dead heart of Africa.

He had received no communication from Elaine since his long-ago letter breaking off the relationship, but he had surreptitiously kept up with her through Embassy friends. He would say he was making inquiries on behalf of her family. That was how he learned she was teaching in Calcutta. Then, two months ago, he got a short letter from a friend at the Embassy in New Delhi, a former colleague who had known them both in Phnom Penh.

"I thought you would want to know," the letter began, and told him that Elaine was dead, drowned at an Indian beach resort. An accident, the friend had stressed. But was it? Elaine was a strong swimmer. That weekend they had spent in Kep they swam to a small island in the Gulf of Siam. He had literally crawled onto the beach, gasping for breath, while Elaine wasn't winded at all. He would have to live with not knowing. A death-in-life sentence.

He turned suddenly toward Sheila, hoping she might think the tears in his eyes were for her, but not really caring.

"You're not going to die, Sheila – don't talk nonsense," he said briskly. "Let's go. I think your plane has landed."

They did not speak again. Just before she climbed the stairway to the plane, he gave her a perfunctory kiss.

As he watched the plane rise into the air, he felt a twinge of guilt.

Maybe I should have told her that Elaine is dead, he thought. It might have dulled her pain.

The Kindness of Strangers

From Julia's journal – Another tidbit from Harper: the Blairs are divorced. I guess Steve finally caught on. Apparently he caught Magda in flagrante delicto...

Magda Blair had always depended on the kindness of strangers – male strangers – and young Father Abruzzi was showing every sign of rising to the occasion.

"You're a widow, Mrs. Blair?" he asked gravely.

She was dressed all in black – the black two-piece dress she had had made in Phnom Penh when Kennedy died, and a black cashmere cardigan "borrowed" from her New York hostess, her increasingly reluctant hostess.

She nodded, though, in fact, Steve Blair was alive and well and living – if you could call it that – in Vientiane.

"Yes," she said, as if choking back tears. "Steven, my late husband, was killed in Laos – by Communists."

Priests hated Communists. She remembered the priests in Hungary, always preaching about the ungodly Reds. Was this the right time to bring up Cardinal Minzenty?

"He was a very brave man," she added, looking the priest in the eyes. Interesting soft brown eyes.

"And, you, Mrs. Blair, are a very brave lady," said Father Abruzzi.

She forced a smile, a brave smile, she hoped, though, in fact, "desperate" might be the more apt word. Steve had come home early one afternoon and found her in bed with a bottle of champagne and the maitre d' from the Hotel Constellation and, quite unreasonably – without even listening to explanations – threw her out with only the clothes she could carry and a one-way ticket to the States.

"I've heard rumors for years, but never believed them – until now," he'd said, more in sorrow than in anger.

And so here she was, stone broke and wearing out her welcome at the apartment of the only friend – no, acquaintance – that she had in New York. Yesterday, she had stopped in a church to rest after a disappointing – no, humiliating – interview at a literary agency that had advertised for a "receptionist with lite typing" – not as "lite" as Magda's however. In the church vestibule, she spotted a notice that a housekeeper/cook was needed for the rectory. Room, board, and a small salary were promised. A place to live and enough money, she hoped, to tide her over until—well, until the next man came along.

"We are three priests," Father Abruzzi was saying. "Father Donlon is semi-retired. Father Cassidy is the pastor, and I am the assistant pastor. We have simple tastes – we like plain food… and our parishioners often bring us casseroles and cakes."

When she was a child, she had often watched – and sometimes helped – the cook make *gulyas* and chicken paprikash.

"Plain food is very good for you," she agreed, with feigned enthusiasm. "But perhaps from time to time I can tempt you with some Hungarian specialties – or Italian dishes. I adore Italian food…"

His eyes lit up. She has guessed right, and surely, she could manage a spaghetti Bolognese.

"About the housekeeping," he said, almost apologetically. "St. Vincent's is a poor parish, but our people love their church. One of our parishioners – a man who works as a janitor in a large office building – volunteers to do most of the heavy work. But you would need to make the beds and do the vacuuming. Is that all right? If you'll pardon me for saying so, Mrs. Blair, you don't look like the sort of woman who's used to doing housework."

"Please, Father Abruzzi," she pleaded. "Give me a chance. It's true, we had servants when I was growing up, but my mother always made me do chores..."

She knew that sounded lame, so she resorted to something that had usually worked with men in the past: tears.

"I am all alone in the world," she sobbed, fishing a linen handkerchief – none of these barbaric paper tissues – out of her purse. "My family perished in 1956..."

Actually, she had no idea what had happened to her family. Magda herself had driven across the border to Vienna with an Austrian businessman who'd bribed the guards.

She snuck a glance at him through her tear-soaked lashes. He looked flustered. Good, she thought, and administered the coup de grace.

"This job is the answer to my prayers," she said. "I came into your church yesterday to ask the Blessed Virgin for help. Then I saw the notice, and I knew she had interceded for me. At least I hoped..."

"Can you give us a reference?" he stammered.

She brightened, wiping away the tears and hoping her face had not turned too red.

"Oh, yes, the woman I am staying with," she said. "She is the wife of a member of the Hungarian delegation to the UN – and a devout Catholic."

He nodded. "Of course, I'll have to check with Father Cassidy…"

She reached over and squeezed his hand, enjoying his blush.

"Oh, thank you, Father," she said. "You will not regret your kindness to a poor, lonely widow."

She splurged on a taxi. After all, she'd soon be earning money, and she hated the subway – where you literally had to rub elbows with all that unwashed humanity. She leaned back in the seat and took out a monogrammed silver compact – a gift of… she couldn't quite remember. The tears had not ruined her makeup, she noted with satisfaction. And her eyes, her large, almost almond-shaped eyes ("She has a touch of the Tartar," Bill Harper had once sniffed, not caring that she overheard. Even so, he was not immune to her charms, she knew) were moist but not red.

By the time the cab reached East 71st Street, she had decided on her exit strategy.

Veronika, her hostess, was seated on the living room couch, drinking tea and looking steely.

She's resolved to throw me out, concluded Magda. The bitch. But Magda was ready for her.

"Darling," she announced, "Like all good things, my visit with you must come to an end. Yes, I met a handsome young man, and, well, I'm going to live with him. And, frankly, darling, you should keep a better watch on your husband. His advances to me were becoming tiresome…"

The look on the other woman's face told her that her barbs had hit home.

"Oh, and this sweater," she added, peeling off Veronika's cashmere cardigan. "There's a moth hole in the sleeve. You really should give it to charity."

Prodigal Moon

From Julia's journal – The tragic events in Cambodia
seem so alien to the place I knew – maybe I really never
knew it at all. I hope some of my friends were among
the refugees who got out. Ket married a French dentist
and now lives in France – thank God. But she wrote that
Ang Khem was among Pol Pot's victims. And I wonder
about Bo. Did the Khmer Rouge find him? Or did he
escape? Poor Mary, not knowing...

Rama's grandparents and his classmates at the Punahou
School called him Ramsey, but his mother never let him
forget that he was named Rama, after a hero-warrior
who fought the monkey army and killed the demons
and that his father was also a hero who was fighting for
good over evil in Cambodia – the land where Rama was
born but which he didn't remember. The only home
he remembered was his grandparents' house in the
Manoa section of Honolulu, near the university where
his grandfather taught. The house had a big garden filled
with ferns and fat red hibiscus flowers and vines that

draped orchids, which reminded Rama of small birds. An old Japanese man tended the garden and didn't like it when Rama climbed the big mango tree at the rear of the yard. He would mutter "*dame, dame.*" Rama didn't understand Japanese, but it was clear that the old man meant he shouldn't climb the tree, so now he only did it on afternoons when the gardener wasn't there. He liked it up there where he could hide in the dark green leaves and see everything that happened in the house and the garden.

On that afternoon he watched as his mother came out of the house carrying an envelope and sat down at the glass-topped table on the lanai. He noticed that her hand shook as she held the envelope up to the light, hesitating. Slowly, she tore it open, then let out a loud cry. He started climbing down from the tree, and his grandmother rushed onto the lanai.

"Mary, dear, what is it?" she asked.

"Oh, mama, it's Bo – he's all right!" his mother cried. "He's in a refugee camp in Thailand, but he's being released. He's coming to us. Rama, your Daddy is coming home."

His grandmother put her arm around his mother's shoulder, but he didn't think she looked very happy. Later, he heard her talking to his grandfather.

"Well," she shrugged. "The prodigal son returns."

"What's a prodigal?" he asked her.

She explained that there was a Bible story about a man who comes home after a long, long time and his family gives a big party.

"Like we'll have when my Daddy comes home?" he asked.

"Well, maybe," his grandmother said, but he noticed that she swallowed hard and quickly started talking about something else.

On the day his father was to arrive, Rama didn't have to go to school. His mother dressed him in the clothes he wore to church on Sundays, and they drove to the airport. On the way, his mother explained that his father had been a refugee, a person who escapes from a country that has a bad government. Then he had spent a long time at a refugee camp, because it took him a long time to find out where they were and to get permission to come to Hawaii. He might not have had enough to eat in the camp, so he might be very thin, even sick. And he probably wouldn't be dressed in good clothes, his mother warned.

As they waited for the plane to arrive, his mother kept getting up and sitting down again, and she held his hand very tightly. When the plane had landed and the people started coming through the door, Rama kept asking his mother, "Is that him?" and she kept shaking her head. Finally, she let go of his hand and ran to greet the man who must be his father. He was tall and very thin, and his shirt was patched and his suitcase was battered. She threw her arms around the man's neck, and tears ran down her cheek.

"Mary, Mary," the man said, patting her hair. Then he gently pushed her away and asked: "Where is my son? Where is Rama?"

Rama came toward them slowly and stuck out his hand, and the man picked him up and held him in the air then put him down and said, "Rama, you're a fine young man, and I am your father."

"Did you really slay the monkey army?" Rama asked shyly, remembering the stories his mother had read to him from the Ramayana.

"I tried," said his father. "I tried very hard."

Rama was a little scared on the way home because his mother kept wiping tears from her eyes and looking at his father and, once, almost bumped into the car ahead of them. But, finally, they were home and he rushed into the house ahead of them to tell his grandparents he had met his father. They were sitting in the living room, reading.

His grandfather stood up and took his father's hand and clapped him on the back.

"Bo, dear," said his grandmother, who remained in her easy chair. "We're so glad you're safe."

They all had dinner on the lanai, and no one talked very much. He guessed his father must be very tired. His mother looked very happy, and kept touching his father's hand.

"Ramsey, you need to go to bed early – it's a school night," said his grandmother. "You can't miss school again."

"Ramsey?" asked his father.

"We thought it best," said his grandmother. "We registered him at school as Ramsey. He's in America now. He needs an American name."

His father was quiet for a minute, and then said, "I see. Well, how about if I call you 'Ram'?"

The boy nodded. 'Ram' sounded grown up.

His mother smiled. "Ram it is," she said.

After dessert, his father said that he was very tired but that he wanted to tell Ram a bedtime story. His mother went to the kitchen to wash dishes, and Ram and his father went down the hall to his bedroom. Ram got under the covers, and his father sat next to him, leaning back against the headboard.

"Tell the one about Rama, please," Ram pleaded.

His father smiled.

"I'm glad your mother told you about him," he said. "Rama was a good man – a prince – and he had a beautiful wife named Sita that he loved very much. He tried to fight against a very bad man, whose name was Ravanna. But the king sent Rama into exile, into a very dangerous forest. He didn't want Sita to go to this dangerous place, so he sent her – and their son—to a safer place across the sea while he fought all the demons in the forest. Finally, when he missed his wife and son so much that he couldn't stand it anymore, Rama prayed to the god of the ocean, Varuna, to build a bridge across the ocean so he could go to Sita…"

Suddenly, Ram noticed that his father's eyes were closed – he had fallen asleep. His mother, who must have been listening at the door, came in and put a finger over her lips and gently pulled his father up by the hand and led him down the hall to her room. His father was still asleep the next morning when Ram left for school.

Ram was happy telling his friends at school that his father had come home, and his mother was always smiling and singing now. Only his grandparents seemed sort of sad, especially his grandmother, who sometimes snapped at his mother.

One night at dinner, Ram asked his grandmother, "When is the welcome party you said we would give for my father?"

"I never said that," said his grandmother, giving him an angry look.

"Your father's going to be too busy for parties," said his grandfather. "He's going to get a job."

"Oh, yes, a party!" said his mother. "So all our friends can meet Bo. What a wonderful idea, Ram."

A few days later, his mother told them her idea for the party. It was to be a *puuhonua* party, she said. The ancient Hawaiians sometimes put returning warriors through a sort of purification ceremony at a place of refuge called a *puuhonua*, she explained. After such a ceremony, it was *kapu* – forbidden – for anyone to harm them or think bad things about them.

"And my daddy was a warrior," said Ram.

"An atonement ceremony," said his grandfather, who knew a lot about Hawaiian history.

"Well, that's what they used to be," agreed his mother quickly. "But since Bo has nothing to atone for, it will just be a celebration –more like a luau, or the big wedding party we didn't have."

His grandmother and grandfather looked at each other strangely, but his mother smiled at him and continued talking about the party plans.

It was to be at the Puu o Mahuka Heiau, a shrine in a big park with nature trails and waterfalls. Ram had been there with his school. And it would be on the next night when the moon would be full.

"A prodigal moon, like you told me about, Grandma?" Rama asked, but his grandmother gave him a dark look and didn't answer.

The day of the party – it was a Saturday – Rama and his mother and father went to the park early and drove up the long, winding road to the temple ruins on top of the hill overlooking the sea. His mother had hired people from a restaurant to make the food, and they were already setting up tables below the temple walls and tending an underground oven, where pork and fish and sweet potatoes were cooking. He and his father both wore Hawaiian shirts, and his mother wore a white muu muu, and all three wore leis of flowers around their necks. When the guests arrived – mostly friends of his mother and his grandparents and some of his classmates and their families – they stood together and greeted everyone and introduced his father. There was a band, and when it got dark, the waiters lit torches and Rama looked up at the full moon.

"Look," he shouted, "it's the prodigal moon that came to welcome my daddy home."

Everyone laughed, and his mother gave him a puzzled look and his grandmother looked embarrassed. When everyone had left, his mother and father and his grandmother and grandfather gathered up the presents people had brought and drove home. Ram was asleep before they even turned into the driveway.

After that, every night at dinner Ram's grandfather would ask: "Any luck today, Bo?" and his father would shake his head. He was trying to find a job, but the newspaper wasn't hiring, and journalism was the only skill he had, he explained. Ram's grandmother bit her lip and looked like she wanted to say something, but she didn't. His mother asked his grandfather if he couldn't find his father a job at the university.

"He knows so much. He could teach the students so much about Asia," she pleaded.

His grandfather said he would try, but he didn't think there were any openings.

After dinner, his father usually went out into the garden to smoke cigarettes because his grandmother didn't allow smoking in the house. One day, his father got a letter. He didn't say what it was, but later, Ram heard his father and mother talking very loud in their bedroom. The next morning at breakfast, his mother's face was red and blotchy.

At dinner, nobody talked much, and when it was Ram's bedtime, his father said he would tell him a story.

"Is it about Rama?" Ram asked as they sat down on his bed.

"Yes," said his father. "About Rama and his cousin. When Rama was exiled to the forest, he sent Sita across the sea where she and his baby son would be safe. But his cousin, whose name was Devi, couldn't escape from the demons, and she hid in the forest with Rama. She helped him fight the monkey army, but when Varuna, the ocean god, built the bridge across the sea so that Rama could go to Sita, the monkey god tied Devi in chains so she couldn't escape. But later, Rama's friend, Hanuman, freed Devi, so she could cross the ocean bridge, too."

His father stopped talking suddenly, and Ram asked, "Is that the end?"

His father laughed.

"No," he said. "That's only the beginning. You have a real-life cousin named Devi. Would you like to meet her? Would you like her to come here?"

"Oh, yes," said Ram, who missed having cousins and brothers and sisters like most of his classmates did. "Will she play ball with me? Can she climb trees?"

"Well, maybe," said his father. "But she's a lot older than you. She'll probably be studying at the university."

Later, he heard loud voices from his parent's bedroom, and his mother, who hardly ever raised her voice, shouted, "I thought things had changed, but you're just like you always were – you and your so-called cousins. I should have known better."

The next morning at breakfast, his parents didn't speak or look at each other, and when Ram came home from school, his mother wasn't at the door to greet him the way she usually was. His grandmother said she was resting and that he shouldn't disturb her and that she didn't know where his father was.

Ram threw down his book bag and went to the back of the garden and climbed up the mango tree. From the branch where he always sat, he could reach some of the mangoes, which had turned from green to orange. Some had big brown spots on them – they were already rotting. He picked one and threw it down on the patio stones. The skin broke, and the yellow insides splattered on the stones. He threw another one down even harder and was glad when the insects and the worms came and attacked the rotting fruit.

Sea Change

From Julia's journal – They still send me the Foreign Service Journal for some reason, and I saw Charlie Sherman's name in the list of "Terminations." I guess they finally caught up with him.

"What's he got that I haven't got?" asked Charlie Sherman, sitting on the balcony of their small apartment with a view of nothing but a parking lot and sipping a gin-tonic – not his first of the day.

"It's what he *hasn't* got, Charlie – a drinking problem," answered Betty, with more regret than bitterness. She had just told him she was going to divorce him and marry a retired Army officer she had met at a bridge tournament.

So, he had been "selected out" once again. That was the genteel euphemism the Foreign Service used for getting rid of dead wood. If you didn't get promoted within a set time, you were let go, fired, involuntarily retired with only a fraction of your pension. This time it was Betty who had "selected him out."

He shook his glass, rattling the ice. It was a habit he had gotten into. In almost all of his posts, there had been a houseboy, or a *boyesse*, or a *babu* to obligingly refill his glass at this signal. Maybe that had been his problem. In the backwater posts of the third world – godforsaken holes like Phnom Penh and Songkla and Surabaya and Cebu – it had been too easy to drink and too hot to do much else. In Phnom Penh, he had played a lot of tennis, and his bastard of a boss had duly noted on his efficiency reports that "Mr. Sherman seems more at home on the tennis courts of the Cercle Sportif than at the office." The narrow-minded bureaucrat failed to mention that Charlie had rubbed elbows with important people at the Cercle, colleagues from other embassies as well as some wealthy Cambodians. At his subsequent posts, he hadn't had the energy even for tennis. He had gained a lot of weight. His face had grown jowly, and his waistline thick. By contrast, Betty, never a beauty, had kept her slim figure, though her face had become drawn, almost gaunt.

Now he was back in Washington, and instead of being sent back out into the field again – he had requested a French-speaking post in Europe – he was being forced to retire at 54. Sent out to pasture.

Field, pasture. What a world of difference! But at least he'd have a pension, though a drastically reduced one.

Then it hit him like a brick. Betty would be getting a big chunk of his pension. Under the new, feminist-driven rules, wives were considered partners. After all, they gave the parties and schmoozed with the ambassador's wife and endured the hardships. He would have to split his meager pension with Betty.

He had to admit she had played the role of Foreign Service wife well. She wasn't a complainer like Tom Grant's bitchy wife, Sheila. She had played bridge with the other wives and entertained visiting press whenever he asked her – which wasn't often since he spent most of his career in backwaters where nothing newsworthy happened. But, after all, she had had servants to do all the work – servants whose wages *he* paid. And she had done more than the required amount of charity work. In Phnom Penh, she had even volunteered at an orphanage. She once brought up the idea of adopting one of the babies. Thank God he had put his foot down. About now, he'd be paying college tuition for the little bastard.

He trudged to the kitchen and made himself another gin-tonic, squeezing the last lime into it. He must remind Betty to buy more limes, he thought. Then he remembered again…

The next day he went to the State Department to sign the papers. The bureaucrats in Personnel were all phony smiles and upbeat remarks about "pursuing other professional options." When he had checked off all the ridiculous boxes and turned in his badge, he dropped by the Foreign Service Lounge, hoping to find an old friend he could go have a drink with. But the room was filled with strangers, young strangers. Lots of young women, too. They seemed to be taking over the Foreign Service. Oh well, maybe they would get divorced some day and have to give half of *their* pensions to their ex-husbands. Sauce for the gander.

He was about to leave when he saw the notice on the bulletin board, half buried in all the offers for trunks and temporary apartments and stuff. "Cruise Lecturers Wanted," it read. "Retired diplomats to lecture on luxury 'learning' cruises. Knowledge of foreign lands required. Asia experience a plus."

Well, he had Asia experience, in spades. He had never bothered to learn the local languages, though. Everybody you needed to deal with spoke English, or, at least French, and his French was pretty good, good enough to meet the minimum requirements of the Foreign Service, at least. And he could say "hello" and "thank you" in Cambodian, Indonesian, Thai and Tagalog.

He went right to one of the phones placed in the lounge for use by officers returned to Washington and called. The interview was set for the next day. He walked back to the apartment with a spring in his step. He had a good feeling about this. He had always been lucky. Lucky Charlie, they had called him at college. He had the kind of luck that somehow always saved his skin when his back was against the wall. When he was fired from that Texas paper, a fraternity brother told him the State Department was recruiting information officers. He bulled his way through the interview and got the job. "Lateral Entry"—no exam.

He couldn't wait to tell Betty. Then he remembered again. Betty was packing. Well, maybe she'd still be there, and he could tell her what she was missing. She had always talked longingly about taking a cruise.

"Let me tell you a little about Orient Pacific Cruises, Mr. –uh, Sherman," said the interviewer next day.

The cruise line didn't have a Washington office, so they were meeting in the recruiter's room at the Roger Smith Hotel.

"We're a small but established line, Panamanian registry, and we specialize in trips for people who want to immerse themselves in the local culture," he recited. "Our passengers are curious, well-educated. They're not traveling just to drink and shop, but to learn about the world. That's not to say that we don't offer opportunities for recreation – and, of course, shopping, especially for the ladies. Are you married, Mr. Sherman?"

"As a matter of fact, I'm separated," Charlie answered. How strange that sounded the first time he said it.

The recruiter brightened.

"Actually, and just between us, we prefer single men," he said. "We get a lot of widows and divorced and single ladies on these cruises. They come primarily for the learning experience, but, in the evenings, they like to relax and have fun on the dance floor. Do you have a tux, Mr. Sherman?"

It was a little frayed, and the white jacket had yellowed a bit, and he hoped he could squeeze himself into it. He'd have to ask Betty where it was.

"All right, here's the deal," the recruiter said, pulling out a contract. "The first cruise is probationary – no pay, just room and board and reasonable bar and laundry expenses. You give a lecture the night before the ship comes into a port – history, culture, points of interest, good things to buy. When we disembark, you lead the passengers on a tour – an insider's tour, from the vantage point of somebody who really knows the territory. At night, you mingle with the guests, dance with the ladies. At the end of the cruise, there's an evaluation. If the passengers like you, and the crew thinks you're okay, we talk about a long-term contract."

Charlie didn't like the "no pay" bit, but what the hell, he didn't have a lot of options. And maybe a cruise was just what he needed. A sea change.

He was hungover when he boarded the ship in Singapore – drinks had been free, even in coach, and he had slung back far too many Singapore slings. Not too hungover though to see that the *China Princess* was a rust bucket. The black-painted hull was pocked with brown, and the once red smokestack had faded to pink. The interior stank of disinfectant and insecticide. His cabin, two floors below deck, was the size of a large closet.

He unpacked and changed into a short-sleeved cotton shirt and went up on deck to stand with the rest of the crew and greet the arriving passengers. Music poured through the loud-speaker system.

"*I'd like to get you*
On a slow boat to China
All to myself alone...."

Oh, brother.

The passengers trudged slowly up the gangplank, lugging their hand luggage. Many used canes. The average age, he estimated, was about 70. Maybe they'd have a burial at sea.

The first night he was to give a general *tour d'horizon* talk in the lounge.

"Nothing too deep," the Purser, who seemed to be his boss, had instructed. "Just fifteen minutes on what the Orient is all about."

As if anybody really knew. Luckily, he had copied some of the Post Reports in the State Department Library, and he was sure he could bull his way through it – even after a couple of gin-tonics in the bar and a copious amount of wine at dinner.

The purser laid it on thick in his introduction, and the passengers – it looked like most of them were there – applauded politely. He launched into his spiel.

"The only people who say the East is inscrutable are those who don't know enough about it," he began. "I'm here to share with you the knowledge I gained during some twenty years' service in the Far East. Let's start by talking about some of the major religions practiced in Asia…"

He started with Buddhism, but soon noticed that some of the passengers were fidgeting and others had actually dozed off. The Purser gave him the high sign, and he quickly wound it up.

"Well, that's probably enough for tonight. I know everybody's jet lagged. I'll be giving another talk just before we arrive at our first port – Manila."

Manila, the Pearl of the Orient. Some pearl. When he was posted in Cebu, he'd get called into Manila for meetings every so often. But all he really saw was the Embassy and, a short cab ride down Dewey Boulevard, the posh Army-Navy Club. He'd sit on the upstairs terrace looking out on the manicured green lawn watching the boats on the bay while the white-jacketed Filipino stewards brought him gin-tonics with those tasty little Calamanci limes they had there.

The audience quickly dispersed, and Charlie gathered his papers. But before he could make his getaway, a woman stopped him.

"Oh, Mr. Sherman," she said, standing in the doorway and effectively blocking his way.

She was tall and thin and spoke with a lock-jawed voice that recalled Katharine Hepburn.

"I'm Ernestine Griswold, and I just wanted to ask you about *yin* and *yang* and just how strong a role you think they play in Asian thought."

What the hell? thought Charlie.

"Well, uh, Miss Griswold," he finally answered. "That's a very interesting question, and I plan to go into that concept in another lecture."

As he hurried away, he thought he detected a knowing smirk. Miss Griswold, he reflected, could turn out to be a pain in the ass.

Garbage floated in Manila Bay, and the stink of sewage hung over the sultry city. From the deck, he could see the Manila Hotel and the Army Navy Club. He'd like nothing better than to repair to the dark, fan-cooled bar of the hotel or the upstairs lounge at the club and spend the day there, but duty called. He had to take the passengers on a history and culture tour. A walking tour, yet! Despite the fact that it was the steamy, pre-monsoon season he'd always hated, when people's nerves were always on edge as they waited for relief from the rains. At least they'd waited until late afternoon, but the heat was still oppressive, and the passengers were already sweating and complaining as he led them through Rizal Park toward the Intramuros, the old city behind the crumbling walls built by the Spanish conquerors in the 1500s.

He led the group through the mercifully shaded arch of the Fort Santiago gate and began his spiel as they continued into the preserved, slightly Disneyesque quarter. *Calesas*, colorfully painted carts drawn by tired-looking horses, plodded along the cobblestone streets.

"Welcome to the Sixteenth Century," he said. "But be careful, those pony carts charge twentieth-century prices. Better to walk. We'll just tour the Cathedral and the Church of San Agustin, and then repair to the Ilustrado Café for light refreshments. And, ladies, there's a wonderful handicraft bazaar adjacent to the café. So, while we gentlemen are partaking, you can shop your little pocketbooks off. And don't worry about a thing. The cruise line has checked out both the café and the shop and you won't get sick and you won't get ripped off."

And the cruise line – and Charlie himself – would get a small kickback.

In the Plaza de Roma, in front of the Cathedral, little brown boys splashed in the fountain under the statues of one of the Spanish kings. God, that looked like fun. Charlie was already winded from walking and sweating like a pig. If only he could rest in the shade by the water. But the group was surging on, and Miss Griswold already had a question.

"Mr. Sherman, is this the original construction?" she asked, eyeing the ornate stone façade with a suspicious air.

"As a matter of fact, Miss Griswold," he answered, "as I was about to explain, this building dates only to 1958. The first cathedral was built here in 1581. It was destroyed and rebuilt several times. During the fierce fighting that took place here during the Battle of Manila in 1945, the 19th century version was leveled to the ground. But this is supposed to be an exact replica. Let's go in. The interior is spectacular."

And cooler, he hoped. The heat was exhausting. Maybe he could take a pew and pretend to pray.

But, inside, the sweetly noxious aroma of incense accosted him. He felt nauseous, light-headed.

He steadied himself by holding on to a marble holy water font.

"Observe the vaulting, and the stained-glass clerestory windows. The chandeliers were brought from Spain," he recited. "I'll just let you explore on your own for a few minutes. Then we'll go across the street to San

Agustin Church, which is the original seventeenth century
building, Miss Griswold."

He sat heavily down in a back pew, while the passengers
walked around the nave, with varying degrees of
enthusiasm. Miss Griswold, he noticed, carried a
guidebook. The better to trip him up, he supposed.
A wedding party was emerging from San Agustin, and
they traipsed merrily across the courtyard to pose for
pictures by the fountain. Charlie led his group into the
ornate, gold-and-white interior. What a setting for a
wedding, he reflected. He and Betty had been married
by a justice of the peace in a small town in west Texas.
She had been a pretty bride despite the homely setting.
She carried a bouquet of bluebonnets they had picked
along the road. He remembered it as if it had been
yesterday.

The group looked at him expectantly.

"This is a true Spanish Baroque church, built in 1607,"
he read from his crib sheet. "Note the *trompe l'oeil*
ceilings. The first Spanish Governor-General of the
Philippines is buried up near the altar."

The passengers trooped up to look at the tomb, and
Charlie plopped heavily down in a pew. He took out a
handkerchief and mopped his face, which was oozing
sweat. He was so tired.

He had almost dozed off when Miss Griswold tapped him on the shoulder.

"Let's climb the tower," she urged. "My guidebook says the view from the top is spectacular."

"Oh, I don't think so, Miss Griswold," he said. "It's a steep climb – there's no elevator. And we need to move on…"

But the other passengers echoed Miss Griswold's enthusiasm. He could let them go on their own and wait from them down the street at the Ilustrado. He badly needed a drink. But, no, something might happen. He'd been told never to leave his group.

"Okay," he reluctantly agreed, and bought the tickets needed to climb the belfry. Miss Griswold bounded ahead of the group. Charlie looked up. The stairs seemed endless. He clutched the shaky rail and began to climb. The stairwell was narrow and totally enclosed and hot as hell. He was out of breath by the first landing and stopped to mop his brow. Most of the passengers were way ahead. Their voices echoed against the thick stone walls. He pressed on, breathing even harder. When he finally reached the top, he could barely talk. He stood for a moment and let the outdoor air cool his face. He looked toward the harbor. He could see the ship, though it seemed awfully far away, shrouded in the humid heat.

God, he'd be glad to climb on the old rust bucket and take a shower and…

"See, wasn't it worth it?" asked Ms. Griswold, spreading her arms out as if she owned the city. "My, Mr. Sherman, your face is awfully red. Are you all right?"

"Fine, fine, Miss Griswold. Too much sun, I guess… Okay, what goes up must go down, right? So, let's move on. Next stop, refreshments and yes, ladies, shopping."

At the Ilustrado, they took several tables by the bar.

"Ilustrado means 'enlightened one,'" he told them. "It was the name the Spaniards gave to the locals who saw the light by embracing Catholicism and learning Spanish."

Miss Griswold asked for tea. Most of the others chose mango or papaya juice. Charlie ordered a gin-tonic.

"With those nice little Calamanci limes, if you've got them."

The waitress brought peanuts with the drinks. God, she's sexy, thought Charlie. So many Filipinas were. They had the Spanish allure with the Oriental submissiveness. That's why Western men went for them. He remembered the little piece he had had in Cebu…

"Is the shop next door a good place to buy capiz?" one of the passengers asked.

"Yes, siree, the best," he replied, jolted out of his meanderings. "First-rate genuine mother-of-pearl, and they have lots of other handicrafts. All guaranteed authentic. It's just across the courtyard. Tell the cashier you're on the *China Princess*, and they'll give you a nice discount."

The bar was quiet after they'd all left, and blessedly cool with the air conditioning and the shade of the trees in the courtyard. He wolfed down the rest of the peanuts – too fast. They sat heavily on his chest, giving him a nagging pain. He ordered another gin-tonic, partly to wash down the peanuts and partly so he could watch the receding rear end of the sexy waitress. But the drink didn't help. The pain in his chest seemed to be getting worse. He should have known better. Nuts always gave him indigestion. When the passengers drifted back in, he could barely rouse himself to count them. They were all laden with purchases: *Capiz* plates, monkey-pod salad bowls, lace blouses, primitive carved wood statues from the outer islands ... what crap! He supposed Betty would get all the junk they had acquired in their various posts. The Bali statues, the Thai silk cushions. The brass candle stands. The Cambodian temple rubbings – the detritus of a failed career and a failed, but not wholly unhappy, marriage. Well, she was welcome to it. But at least he now had an excuse to take the passengers and their purchases back to the ship via taxi.

When he was finally back in his cabin, he threw himself down on the bunk. He wanted to take a shower first, but he didn't have the strength to take off his clothes and walk into the tiny bathroom. He fell asleep, waking only when he heard the first bell for dinner. He felt a little better. That nap had been just what he needed. He showered quickly and dressed. Thank God he didn't have to squeeze himself into his tux again. This was Philippines Night, and everyone was supposed to dress the part. Luckily, he had been able to find his old *Barong Tagalog*, the loose white embroidered shirt that was acceptable formal wear here.

The dinner was served buffet style. It was all Filipino food but whitewashed for the American palate. He put a few *lumpia* on his plate and a couple spoonsful of rice. He suddenly felt vaguely nauseous. Maybe those *Calamanci* limes in the gin-tonics at the café had been off. Or the ice. He should have known better than to trust the ice in a country like this.

He picked at his food and managed to keep up a conversation with his tablemates. Then the orchestra started up. Oh, God, he would have to dance. Part of the *noblesse oblige* he had agreed to. Maybe he should dance now and get it over with, then sneak away to his bunk.

He saw Miss Griswold across the room, wearing some sort of Filipina peasant costume. She looked ridiculous, but at least she wasn't fat like so many of the other women passengers. If she stepped on his feet, he'd survive. He ambled toward her.

"Miss Griswold, may I have the honor?" he asked.

"Why, Mr. Sherman, of course," she said, rising from her chair.

Fortunately, it was a slow dance, a foxtrot, which he knew how to do.

On the dance floor, he felt a little dizzy. So many turns. And the pain in his chest had come back – with a vengeance – and was shooting down his left arm. He clutched Ms. Griswold's shoulder. Her smile turned to alarm.

"Mr. Sherman, are you quite all right?" she asked.

He smiled, and tried to answer, but there was a loud ringing in his ears, and he couldn't get the words out.

"Betty," he mumbled, then remembered.

Maybe the ball was over. Maybe there really would be a burial at sea. Maybe the joke was on him.

He threw back his head and laughed – his last.

. .

Nothing Gold Can Stay

From Julia's journal – Received a hand-painted postcard of what looks like a marsh, from Harper, with a cryptic note saying he had retired to Cape Cod – "he" not "we." Hope that doesn't mean Helene has left him –he'd be lost...

After Helene left him – vanishing into the mists of China – Bill Harper retired to a cottage on Cape Cod Bay and bought an Irish setter, whom he named Isolde so he could say *"Mein irisch kind, wo weilest du?"* –the hauntingly plaintive air from Wagner's opera. Every morning, he would put the dog on the front seat of the car and drive across the narrow peninsula to Nauset Beach and let her run along the shore, chasing the gulls and dancing in and out of the water to retrieve whatever jetsam he threw for her.

This morning, the wind was whipping the sand into a frenzy, stinging his eyes with sand and salt so he could barely see. Or was it tears – tears of regret for the beauty of the beach and the sky and the dog, of the world that would soon be lost to him?

In the afternoon, he followed his usual routine, setting up his easel on the deck and trying to capture the afternoon light – that last, heart-rending gasp of gold illumining the marsh before the scene faded, and the slowly descending darkness sucked the light and the life out of it. Nothing gold can stay, he reflected wryly. A bit like himself – his once dark blonde hair had long since faded to a dead gray. A bit like his life.

He squeezed out some quinonochrome gold and made a wash and gently brushed some on the paper to illustrate the light, but the yellow-gold paint mixed with the purples and greens of the marsh and muddied, creating what his former art teacher would have called "a pig's breakfast." The golden moment had eluded him once again.

Sighing, he put the paints away, mixed himself a Scotch and water and returned to the deck to wait for David. His oldest son, his and Helene's, an Assistant Professor of Far East Studies at Harvard, was coming to take the dog.

Isolde, lying on the deck and twitching with inscrutable dog dreams, woke up instantly when the car approached. Recognizing David, she stopped barking and wagged her tail, thumping it against the railing.

Funny, thought Harper watching his son approach, the only thing Asian about him is his walk. David had Caucasian features, but walked like a Chinese scholar, which he was, in a sense.

"Hi, Dad," he said somberly.

"Hi, son," he said. "Want a drink?"

"No, thanks," David demurred, probably thinking of the long drive back to Cambridge. Isolde gravitated to the younger man's side, putting her head on his knee.

"*La donna è mobile*," said Harper, but glad of it. Isolde would have a good home.

"Any word from your mother?"

An unfortunate segue but David merely shook his head.

When he was posted to Hong Kong, he knew it was a dead end, a consolation prize for never having been made an ambassador. The conventional wisdom was that China could take Hong Kong with a phone call, if the Communist giant didn't want to wait until the 99-year lease was up. But Helene was in heaven. They found an apartment overlooking Repulse Bay, but Helene spent most of the time visiting her family. Her mother still lived in an old house on the Peak, and her brother had a penthouse high above Deep Water Bay. Then there were cousins scattered all over the place, in the New Territories and even in Guandong province in the real China.

It was one of these cousins who had approached Helene. Would Bill be willing to share certain information with him? Nothing sensitive – just insights into the Consulate-General's thinking on certain issues, economic issues mostly. He would be promoting good relations between China and the United States, and they would make it worth his while.

Naturally, Bill refused. In no uncertain terms.

But Helene saw things differently.

"It's not like before," she said. "China and the United States are friends, now. And we have all these tuition payments coming up…"

It was true. Bill's family trust, which had cushioned their Foreign Service life for so long, had run dry, and Hong Kong was very expensive…

In the end, he agreed to pass on some papers. Nothing substantive. Mostly papers marked "Limited Official Use" or "Confidential." Certainly nothing marked "Secret" or "Top Secret." Stuff they easily could have learned from *The New York Times* or even *The China Morning Post*, he rationalized. Modern espionage, like piracy, seemed to be mainly a matter of desk work.

The only cloak-and-dagger aspect of it was the drop, a trash can in back of a Chinese restaurant in North Point. Throughout his career, there had been rumors– totally unfounded – that he was an undercover CIA operative. Ironic that he was finally, in a sense, fulfilling that myth. But, toward the end of his tour, he began to have the uneasy feeling he was being followed. He said that to Helene, and shortly after that, she told him she was going to visit a cousin in the New Territories. She never returned.

He sent in his retirement letter and bought the old, brown-shingled cottage with the last of his ill-gotten gains and waited. He knew it was only a matter of time.

The government had been gentlemanly about it. They allowed him to plead guilty to only one count of espionage – what a glamorous, romantic word for such a tawdry, pedestrian deed. His lawyer had negotiated what he assured Harper was a good deal: thirty years in a minimum-security prison, with possibility of a parole in twenty.

He laughed at the picture of himself as an 84-year old ex-con, squinting into the sunlight.

His lawyer was coming in the morning and would drive him to the Federal Building in Boston, where he would surrender.

"David, you should go," he urged. "It's getting dark."

He stood, and his son embraced him, awkwardly. They had never been a physically demonstrative family.

He saw tears in his son's eyes as David put the dog on her lead and walked her to his car. Isolde seemed confused. She looked back at Harper inquiringly. Then, at his benedictory wave, hopped into the car – a new adventure.

The night air was cold, but Harper stayed on the deck. Darkness was obscuring the marsh. He regretted that he had never captured it in the glory of its magic, golden hour, and never would.

Perhaps there would be art classes at Allenwood, he thought. He heard there were activities like that, a sort of therapy.

But golden afternoon light, he suspected, gazing at the last faint outlines of the marsh, would be in short supply.

Music Lessons

From Julia's journal – Just reread Fitzgerald's Tender Is the Night. The ending made me think of Jake. Dick Diver keeps drifting westward, to smaller and smaller towns. That's how I picture Jake...

When Barb was offered the assistant principal job in Sioux Falls, Jake O'Donnell decided he had had enough of teaching. It wasn't the kids. They were great, especially the immigrants from Asia who had begun to filter into the Minnesota prairie. But bureaucracies were the same everywhere, he concluded, and the education bureaucracy was, if anything, more stultifying than the one he had run afoul of in the Foreign Service. So, after they moved west – bringing their furniture in a U-Haul truck to a small house they had rented, sight unseen, near Barb's school— he started looking for a job. There wasn't much of a market for former diplomats who spoke Cambodian and French, but he parlayed his teaching experience into a job selling retirement annuities to teachers. He liked the job – he liked teachers and, God knows, they needed retirement income —but it kept him on the road, away from home.

Barb was a trouper, of course – always had been. When he had come home after his less-than-graceful exit from the Foreign Service, she had been understanding. She wouldn't have wanted that kind of life, she said. She already had her teaching credential, and he got his over the summer in an accelerated program – they really needed teachers in rural Minnesota. They were married that fall, and both got teaching jobs in a small town on the prairie. Barb always said hers was only temporary – she wanted to stay home when the children came. But children never came. Barb had gone to a doctor to get checked out, and there was nothing wrong. It must have been him, he thought.

Jake had wanted to adopt a Vietnamese child, but, surprisingly, Barb was adamantly against it – almost as if she were jealous of his past. They put themselves on the waiting list for a white, American baby, but the adoption agency never called, and they didn't talk about it anymore.

His territory covered all the Plains States, which meant long distances on straight, dull roads where you could see your destination long before you got there. That about summed up his life, he thought, straight and dull and colorless with no unknown destinations, no surprises.

Even the landscape was painted in washed-out colors. He missed the gaudy melon flower of the tropics.

Dusk was falling when he saw Lincoln, Nebraska, rising up before him like a mirage, the low-slung cityscape with the jutting Capitol dome. Gratefully, he turned off the interstate and made his way toward the downtown hotel where he usually stayed. He checked in and changed clothes and went out to look for a drink before dinner. He hated the sterility of hotel bars.

He found a place that looked inviting and unpretentious on North Ninth Street, and as soon as he went in, he saw her. Nicole, the Vietnamese bar girl he had known in Phnom Penh –who through no fault of her own may have cost him his Foreign Service career— was behind the bar, chatting up a customer. When she heard the door shut, she looked up and saw him, too.

"Jake," she said, almost in a normal voice, as if he had just walked into the bar where she had worked in Phnom Penh, the Chez Tyna, before she married one of the young Marine guards from the Embassy.

She had aged badly. There were dark circles under her eyes that her heavy makeup couldn't hide. Her face was drawn, and her body much thinner. And she had dyed her hair an artificial-looking red, probably to hide the gray. He had changed, too, and he saw the changes reflected in her steady gaze. His receding hairline had receded completely – he was bald. And the sedentary life, and all those hours in the seat of a car, had thickened his waistline and given him the beginnings of a paunch.

"'Of all the gin joints in all the towns in all the world...'" he began.

But the allusion was lost on her and she looked puzzled, maybe a bit hurt, so he changed the subject.

"*Ça va, Nicole?*" he asked, and she came around from behind the bar and threw her arms around his neck, and for a moment, he lost himself in the smell of stale cigarettes and liquor and the sweet, heady perfume she still wore.

"*Il a été longtemps,*" she answered, noncommittally.

It *had* been a long time.

She led him to a small table away from the bar, then went to fetch drinks. Scotch for him, his regular drink in the old days, and for herself she brought a glass filled with what smelled like gin. In Phnom Penh, she had drunk very little – mainly plain water dyed green so the bar could charge the male customers for it.
"*Santé,*" she toasted, touching his glass with hers.
"To old times, and old friends," he responded.

She smiled, nervously. They both seemed reluctant to speak of either the present or the past. Finally, he ventured, "How is Chuck?"

"Ah, Jake, it did not work for Chuck and me," she replied. "When we were in Manila, when we first got married, it was good – wonderful. But, then, we came here. He was so happy to see his friends, his family, I was not so important anymore. And they did not like me. Then Eddie was born. We named him Edward, after Chuck's father. But Eddie looks so much like me. They didn't really want him as a grandchild. Now, Chuck has an American wife and an American son. He lives in Grand Island and works for his father, selling John Deere tractors. Eddie lives here, with me. Chuck doesn't come to see him much."

"I'm sorry," he stammered, not really surprised, and downed the rest of his Scotch. Nicole went for refills, chatting with the lone customer at the bar, who was getting up to leave.

"And your sister?" he asked when she sat down at the table again. "And the other children?"

When she went to Manila to join Chuck, Nicole left her two older children in the care of her sister with vague promises that she would send for them later.

Again, a shadow crossed her face.

"My sister," she began. "I'm not sure where she is. She had to leave Phnom Penh – things were not good for Vietnamese there. She always said it was a mistake to marry Chuck. I didn't want to admit she was right, so I never wrote her after the divorce... My daughter would be almost grown up by now. I'm sure she is beautiful. I hope she is not working as a bargirl..."

She shrugged and took a swig of gin.

"But I have Eddie," she said, brightening. "He is a wonderful boy, smart in school. And he loves music. I want to give him music lessons. Chuck thinks that's crazy, for a boy, so he won't pay. I can't afford it now, but one day... You must meet him, Jake. You would like him."

"You're lucky. I always wanted children," Jake said, gazing into his Scotch. "But Barb and I never had any. Something wrong with me, I guess – I wasn't equipped to have children..."

She took his hand, and her eyes filled with tears. "No, Jake, that's not true," she said, looked into his eyes. "I know, I know."

He stared at her, open-mouthed, remembering that terrible, long-ago trip to Kompong Speu, to the abortionist.

"You mean..." It came out as a hoarse whisper as the truth dawned: It had been his incipient child left behind at that sordid clinic.

She nodded, then dried her tears.

"Come on," she said, taking his hand. "I'll close early. There won't be any more customers tonight. You can come to my place and meet Eddie."

She turned off the lights and locked the bar, and he followed her car to the rundown garden-apartment complex near the university where she and Eddie lived. He thought briefly of her small room on the outskirts of Phnom Penh where he had taken her after the abortion so long ago. Nicole had gotten rid of the incipient child that might have clouded her future and she abandoned her older children. All so she could marry an American Marine, who dumped her. But she was tough, Nicole was, and she had Eddie. Maybe that was enough.

"Mostly students live here," she said apologetically, as they climbed the stairs to her second-floor apartment." The carpet was worn, and the odors of stale food seeped from under the doors of the other apartments, but Nicole's place looked neat and clean. Temple rubbings from

Angkor Wat hung on the walls, and a black lacquer coffee table sat in front of a rattan sofa. In a corner, a small cinnabar altar held a porcelain Buddha, whose garishly painted lips smiled down on a bowl filled with ripening mangoes. A spent joss stick gave off the sickly-sweet aroma he remembered from Buddhist shrines and Hindu temples.

"I'm back in Asia," he said.

"Chuck and I bought furniture in Manila, but when we got here, he thought it didn't look right," she said.

Like Nicole, he thought. She didn't look right here, either. He felt very sorry for her and took her in his arms. She melted against him for a moment, then disengaged herself.

"Eddie," she called out, but her soft voice was drowned out by the loud volume of a television behind a closed door adorned with a Grateful Dead poster.

She knocked and opened the door and spoke to the boy, who dutifully turned off the cop show he had been watching and emerged into the hall. He looked about nine or ten with delicate features like Nicole's and almond-shaped dark eyes. Only his build and height betrayed some American roots.

"Hello, Eddie," Jake said. "I'm Jake. I'm an old friend of your Mom's."

The boy proffered a limp hand and gave him a surly look, and it occurred to Jake that Eddie was probably often introduced to friends of his Mom who came for late night visits.

"Have you finished your homework, Eddie?" Nicole asked. "You know you're not supposed to be watching television. Anyway, it was too loud – the neighbors will complain."

The boy excused himself, ostensibly to do homework, but soon Jake could hear the television again, though at a lower volume. Jake sat on the couch, and Nicole poured drinks from a rattan bar in the corner of the small room and joined him.

"To old times," she said, clinking her glass against his. "Remember the time you took me to that snooty French restaurant and the maître d' turned up his nose at me, but you kept saying '*Madame voudrait cela*," or "*Madame n'aime pas ça,*" – treating me like a lady. I loved you for that, Jake…"

He remembered she had ordered a dish of little birds and cracked their small, brittle bones and ate the meat off them. Afterward, every time he embraced her, he had an eerie feeling that her bones, too, might break.

"We had good times, Nicole," he said, and memories of the time and the place where they had known each other flooded back.

The emerald green of the rice paddies that lined the roads. The orange flame trees fluttering against the cloudless blue sky. The whoosh of the wheels of the *cyclo-pousses* in the rain-soaked streets. The sweet smell of opium pipes at Madame Phuong's. The beautiful young Vietnamese girls riding to church on bicycles, their pastel *hai-daos* fluttering in the soft breeze.

His eyes misted over, and he saw her through the mist and reached for her.

"Come," she said, and led him into the bedroom. The bed was neatly covered with a pink satin quilt, which she peeled back. He lay on the sheets, suddenly very tired, while she gently undressed him. Then, with a quick motion, she took off her own clothes, and even in the dark, he could see that she was old. Her collar bone stood out like a skeleton's, and her small breasts sagged down on her prominent ribs. She lay down on top of him and began working her lips down his body, muttering endearments in barely audible French.

He was tired, and the Scotch had taken its toll, and he could hear the television in the next room – her son's room. His penis remained limp, and all he really wanted was to hold her in his arms and sleep and dream of the past.

"Jake, you are tired," she said. "Here, let me…"

"No, Nicole," he said, taking her hand away and kissing it.

"It wouldn't be good. I've been driving all day – I'm exhausted. Let's just remember the times we had."

He kissed her tenderly, then disengaged.

"I need to go," he said. "I have an eight o'clock breakfast with teachers, and I have to prepare."

He took his clothes into the bathroom and dressed quickly, then took two fifty-dollar bills out of his wallet.

Nicole almost cringed when he handed them to her.

"Oh, Jake, no…" she protested.

"Please," he said. "For the music lessons, for Eddie." "Eddie," she repeated, and her smile made her look almost as beautiful as she once was. "Jake, I knew back then you would never marry me. With Chuck, I had a chance. That's why..."

"It's all right, Nicole," he said, and kissed her on the forehead.

She took the money and placed it on the nightstand, and he turned and left the apartment quietly, still hearing the sound of the television from Eddie's room. When he opened the building door, the cool air of the Nebraska night brought him back to the present, and as he drove back to the hotel in the dark, quiet streets, he thought of Barb.

Her birthday was next week, and she had always wanted diamond earrings. On his last trip, he had seen a small pair of studs in the window of a jewelry shop in Kansas City. The jeweler said he could have them for $100. He had drawn the money out of his savings account and was going to pick them up on his way through. He could picture her face when she saw the small velvet box he would leave on the breakfast table. Instead, he would send Barb a dozen long-stemmed red roses, as he did every year. Barb loved roses. The earrings would have to wait. Barb would understand.

She always did.

Alien Corn

From Julia's journal – I had hoped to see Ket when we're in Paris. We could rent a car and go out to Rouen and see the cathedral and take her to lunch. But the letter I sent to the last address I had for her, in a small town near Rouen, came back marked "inconnue" – unknown –not stamped by the post-office but written in a spindly, old-lady scrawl...

In the fall, there were fewer and fewer fresh fruits and vegetables in the open-air market in the cathedral square where Ket always stopped before she boarded the bus for the village. Opening her string bag, she selected a few apples. She never developed a taste for this ubiquitous Norman fruit. Once, in Paris, when she was desperately homesick for Phnom Penh, she had bought some mangoes, and Paul scolded her for the extravagance. But apples would do to make a tarte for dinner. A tarte for a *ménage à trois* – her husband, Dr. Paul Garcelon, herself and, of course, her *belle-mère*.

She thought fleetingly of her French girlfriend back in Phnom Penh, a girl who had married a Cambodian student she had met in Paris. In France, he had been *"le plus gallant des gallants"* but when they went to Phnom Penh, they had to live with his family, and she became a handmaiden to her mother-in-law, while her husband spent his evenings on the town. Ket could not say that about Paul. He had no interest in night life, not that there was any in a Norman village. But they lived with his widowed mother, and Ket, who had always had a maid growing up, did all the cooking and housework. And Paul was different here. In Phnom Penh, during their brief courtship, he had showered her with candy and *marrons glacés* and flowers and taken her to fine restaurants. Here, he watched every franc she spent and deferred to his mother in all things.

Paul had been her family's dentist. He had gone out to Indochina with the army but had stayed on after independence and set up practice in a comfortable villa on the Boulevard Norodom. She had known him since she was little more than a child. He was twelve years older. But she'd seem him rarely. He was not in her set, at all. In fact, he rarely went out but stayed at home with his books.

"He's very shy," her mother had said when she'd come home after a dental appointment and announced that she had invited Dr. Garcelon to dinner. Ket was surprised. Her mother rarely entertained, and certainly not foreigners, not since her husband had died many years before. She should have suspected something.

Her sister was at university in the U.S., so it was just the three of them. Her mother had steamed a whole fish, and Paul ate heartily, grateful, he said, for a home-cooked meal. After dinner, they sat on the small balcony, and Paul sipped a cognac her mother had offered to him, but only to him.

"I don't know how I will get along without you, Dr. Garcelon," her mother said. Ket hadn't known it before, but the dentist was returning to France, leaving his practice to a young Cambodian who had trained in France. Most foreigners had already left Cambodia, fearful of a takeover by the rebels.

"Dr. Luong is very competent," the dentist replied. "I have taught him everything I know. You will be in good hands."

Ket wondered at her mother's naiveté. If the rebels took over, dentistry would be the least of her problems.

"And, of course, I worry most about Ket," her mother continued. "She worked for the American ambassador, you know, and then for the Sihanouk government. I fear there will be no place for her in the new Cambodia…"

She had gone to the Embassy straight from the Lycée Descartes. An old friend of her father's, who worked at the Ministry of Foreign Affairs, had recommended her as a translator – with the clear, but unstated, understanding, that she report back to him on what was going on at the Embassy. Nothing secret, really, just gossip –whatever morsels she happened to pick up. When the Embassy packed up and left, she went to work for the Ministry, until the change…

"Nor for you, Madame, as the widow of a high government official," Dr. Garcelon was saying. "You should leave, both of you."

"I am an old woman. No one will bother about me. And my family graves are here. I will stay," she said. "I would like Ket to emigrate, but we have little money. My government pension was stopped. …Ah, but enough of this. Tell us your plans."

He planned to practice dentistry in Paris, he told them. An old Army colleague, another dentist, had invited him to join his practice.

Paris, thought Ket, wistfully. But after Dr. Garcelon had left – rather hastily – she exploded at her mother.

"That was so obvious – you practically offered me to him," she shouted. "He's old and dull. I don't want to marry him. "

She shuddered at the thought of it. She was vaguely repelled by his washed-out blue eyes and his pale skin and thinning red hair.

Her mother looked at her, steely-eyed.

"Have you thought of the alternative?" she asked, and Ket was silent.

She was twenty-nine, long past marriageable age in Cambodia.

Rumor was that the rebels, who called themselves the Khmers Rouges, were advancing on the capital.

The next day, Dr. Garcelon's driver delivered a note thanking them for dinner and inviting them both to dinner at La Sirène, the restaurant behind the Hotel Royale. When he arrived to collect them that evening, her mother pleaded a headache, and he and Ket dined alone. Then there were other dinners and films at the Ciné-Luxe, and one night, as he parked his Citroen in front of her apartment building, he cleared his throat noisily and said, "Mademoiselle – Ket – I am older than you, but I am in good health and I have developed a strong affection for you. I know this is sudden, but, due to political events, I must book my return to France very soon. I would very much like to take you with me, as my wife. I would, of course, take your dear mother as well."

"She won't go," Ket said quickly.

He smiled. He looked almost attractive when he smiled.

"My dear Ket, does that mean that you will?" he asked.

She nodded, and he embraced her, rather awkwardly.

They were married in a government office – she was Buddhist and he was Catholic – with only her mother and Dr. Luong in attendance. On their brief honeymoon, at the Auberge de Kep, he proved an inept lover and expressed shock and disappointment that she had not been a virgin.

She shrugged.

"I am twenty-nine," she said, wondering if his ineptness indicated that he, at forty-one, had been a virgin.

At the airport, before they boarded the Air France flight for Paris, both Ket and her mother cried.

"*Partir, c'est mourir un peu*," her mother whispered and pressed into her hand the watch her father had gotten when he retired from the government.

"You will visit us often," Paul said, though all of them knew she would not.

From Orly, they took a taxi to the apartment Paul's friend had rented for them in the 18th *arrondissement* near the Gare du Nord, a small furnished studio on the *troisième étage* of an old building that looked out on a courtyard filled with garbage cans.

"Of course, this is only temporary – until I get my practice started," said Paul, sensing her disappointment.

"I'm happy to be here," she assured him.

Maybe I'm just tired, she told herself, and she made up the bed in the alcove and crawled under the duvet and slept for ten hours.

It was cold in Paris, and she had no winter clothes, she told Paul. He showed her how to use the Metro and gave her some money – not enough, she found, when she got to the Galeries Lafayette. She had barely enough for a sweater and a warm coat. As she went down the escalator with her purchases, she spotted Denise Foletti, splendidly dressed, at the perfume counter. Although they had never been close friends, Ket was so glad to see someone from home that she greeted Denise effusively.

"*Ket, ma chère, toi ici!*" cried the other, kissing her on both cheeks and inviting her to take a coffee. "I want to hear about everyone in Phnom Penh – *et toi-même* of course."

They went to a nearby café, and Denise ordered an espresso while Ket, worried that she might not have enough to cover the coffee and her Metro fare home, settled for a coffee.

Denise congratulated Ket on her marriage to Dr. Garcelon, who had been her dentist, too, but talked mainly about herself. Denise had married Charles Hourani, the Moroccan diplomat they had both known in Phnom Penh, and lived with him in Montparnasse. She still worked for Air France, flying the Paris/Hong Kong run. She had, she confessed, a lover in Hong Kong, a rich Chinese who gave her jewelry that she hid in a bank vault.

"My retirement fund," she said, and laughed. "Or my escape fund."

Ket was shocked at this bald confession, though she had never liked – or trusted – Hourani. He had treated her friend Julia badly.

"We must all have dinner together some night," Denise said as they parted – to Ket's relief, she had picked up the check – but they didn't exchange telephone numbers, so Ket knew it would never happen.

They stayed in the small apartment all winter. Paul went to his dental office every day, but never said anything about getting a bigger place. He was very conservative with money, which was understandable given he was just starting his practice here. Despite the cold, Ket had to get out, so she started going to the cinema in the afternoons. One day, she returned from a matinee, and Paul was already home, looking unhappy.

"My partner – I thought he was my friend – says there is not enough work for both of us," he announced. "He also had the temerity to criticize my methods as old-fashioned. I have decided that we should return to Normandy, to my home. My mother is old, and she has a large house. We can live with her, at least while I can get settled. Dentists are needed – and appreciated – in the country."

Normandy. Wasn't that where Madame Bovary lived? Ket had just seen the film and cried at the ending.

"But I was thinking I could get a job here in Paris… maybe as a translator. I could help until things got better for you," she offered.

But the decision had been made.

"You will have enough to do," he said, firmly. "*Maman* is old, and weak."

Weak, she was not, Ket swiftly found, at least not in will. As soon as they arrived at the farmhouse – a half-hour taxi ride from the train station in Rouen – her *belle-mère* took firm charge of them both, treating Paul like a child and Ket like a servant. Every week, she doled out a small amount of money to Ket for household expenses, and expected her to account for every *sou*. Paul set up a practice in an office in the center of the village, which he shared with a doctor, but, except for brief shopping expeditions, Ket was at home and at her mother-in-law's beck and call. She was a cold woman, Ket decided, showing only minimal affection toward her son and none at all toward Ket, whom she probably looked down upon as a "person of color." She missed her own mother more every day.

And she found the city cold, unwelcoming. When they arrived, Paul had shown her around, proudly pointing out the forbidding, dark gray stone cathedral and the tower where the young Joan of Arc had been imprisoned, before she was burned to death.

She had shuddered. Joan of Arc, Madame Bovary. Rouen was a city of death for women.

In the cosmopolitan melting pot of Paris, Ket had not felt out-of-place. Since her *lycée* days, when she decided she wanted to look more like her French classmates, she had curled her naturally straight and thick black hair every morning with a curling iron. And she'd always been careful to stay out of the sun, so her skin was a Mediterranean olive, like that of many Parisians. But, in Normandy, most people were fair-skinned, like Paul.

She was not the only "person of color" in the area, she learned one day when her mother-in-law had a visitor, another old lady. Ket served them tea, then retreated to her room. But when she went back to the parlor to clear up the tea things, she heard them talking about how refugees from Southeast Asia were flooding the region, even sending their children to French schools.

"*Figurez-vous*!" her mother-in-law's friend exclaimed, indignantly.

When Paul returned that evening, Ket looked at the newspaper, which he always brought home but in which she normally took scant interest. An education center had been set up in Rouen to tutor refugee children so they could enter French schools.

As soon as she read that, she realized how homesick she was. Maybe there would be people she knew – or who could tell her about her mother. She was so worried.

She jotted down the address of the education center and, the next day, she took the bus into Rouen and found it, in a converted warehouse on the outskirts of the city.

The Director was pleased to see her.

"Ah, *madame*, you are Cambodian, *parait-il*. Do you speak Khmer?"

"*Bien sûr*," she replied, and he quickly offered her a job.

"Not as a teacher, *entendez-vous*," he clarified.

All the children would be "mainstreamed," and speak only French, which they would learn from native French speakers. But, at least at the beginning, there was a need for aides, to translate, to explain to the parents what they must do.

He seemed flustered, overwhelmed by the daunting task that had been thrust upon him.

She quickly accepted, and he named an hourly rate, a low hourly rate, but she would have done it for free. Later, when she'd decided how to use the money, she wished she'd asked for more. He would have agreed, she felt sure.

That evening, she told Paul about her job, and as she expected, he was angry.

"My mother needs you here," said her husband.

But she gained support from an unexpected quarter.

"How much will you be paid?" asked her mother-in-law, her eyes glinting with greed.

Thinking quickly, Ket named half of the actual, meager figure, but they apparently thought that was all she was worth.

Paul acquiesced.

"You will, of course, turn your earnings over to *maman* for the household expenditures, and you will continue your household duties."

She nodded, ostensibly obedient.

The next week, she rose early, prepared breakfast and cleaned up the dishes before boarding the bus into Rouen. When she arrived, a large crowd of people had gathered outside the center, waiting for the doors to open. There were Cambodians, some Laotians, a few Vietnamese, and a smattering of Africans.

"*Sohm toh, pardon,*" she said, as she squeezed through to the door and showed the pass she had been given.

Inside, the director explained the procedure and gave the teachers their assignments. The children would first be tested in French. Any with a reasonable facility would be put in an accelerated class. The others would be divided into age groups. Ket would help the teacher of the eight-to-ten-year-olds.

The warehouse had been partitioned to create classrooms, and as Ket looked for hers she saw a vaguely familiar face.

"Mademoiselle Ket!" cried the man with the familiar face, and she remembered who he was.

"Monsieur Prak Youn," she cried, inordinately glad to see him.

He had been the Khmer teacher at the Lycée Descartes. The *lycée* had had a strictly French curriculum, awarding the French "bac," preparing the children of expatriates for the French university system. But, under political pressure, the *lycée* had hired a teacher of the Cambodian language and offered it as an elective. Ket had not taken it, of course, but some of her friends had, and she was frequently called upon to help with homework, but she had had little contact with Monsieur Prak Youn.

"Please, have a coffee with me after classes," he asked, and she agreed, calculating that she would have a few minutes before the bus left for the village.

She was tired by the end of the day, and emotionally drained. One of the little girls in her class had cried and clung to her mother, until Ket and the teacher pulled her away.

"Please," the mother begged Ket in Khmer. "She has lost her father. She has nightmares about losing me. Be gentle with her."

The little girl, whose name was Chou, then clung to Ket.

"One day, many trucks came into the city," she confided. "Men in black pajamas got out of the trucks and came into our building. They had big, long knives. They made everyone go out on the street. They took my father and some of the other men away. Then they made the rest of us get into the trucks, and we drove to the countryside to a sort of prison. We had to work in the fields, and there was never much to eat, and if we cried, they beat us with sticks…"

"It's all right," Ket tried to console her. "It's over now."

But Ket was distraught. If the Khmers Rouges had done that to small children, what might have they done to her mother.

Afterwards, she walked with Prak Youn to a café nearby.

"You are tired, *mademoiselle*. Perhaps you'd rather…"

"No," she said. "It's all right. I want to hear about Phnom Penh. My mother is there…"

He looked grave.

"I was fortunate," he said. "I had gone to Battambang to spend the Lunar New Year with my family. When I heard what was happening in Phnom Penh, I walked through the mountains to the Thai border. I knew that, as a teacher in a French *lycée*, I would be a target. But my parents said they were too old to leave, and my brother's wife was pregnant. I, too, am worried."

On payday, she went to a bank in Rouen to cash her check and to set up an account in her own name. Remembering what Denise had said, she privately called it "my escape fund." She put half the amount of her pay in the account and dutifully turned the other half over to her mother-in-law.

They took to meeting at the café most afternoons. Ket told herself it was to exchange information, but in truth, she found she was attracted to him. At last, she had someone to talk to about home. In the beginning, Paul was that person. He had known more of her friends than Prak Youn had – he was closer to her social set. But, here, Paul was a stranger. In his mother's house, he was his mother's son, and she was little more than a servant. And he never touched her, saying that lovemaking would disturb his mother. She had been relieved, at first, but lonely, too.

Ket enjoyed the children. Maybe she could study to be a real teacher, she thought. When one of them was pronounced ready to be mainstreamed into a regular French school, she knew she would miss the child. Youn said the same. He was an aide – an aide, although he had been a full-fledged teacher at the *lycée* – to a teacher of older boys, the lucky few who had escaped the labor camps.

When winter came, they sat inside at the café, as near to the heater as they could. Neither was used to the French winter, and Ket was more and more homesick. Youn would walk her to the bus stop afterward, and, one day, he started holding her hand. It felt good, although she worried that someone from the village might see her.

One afternoon, it snowed very heavily, and the bus never came.

"I have a room near here," said Youn, and she nodded. She called Paul's office from the café and left a message with his assistant that she was spending the night with another teacher. Youn led her up shabby staircase, and heated soup on an electric hot plate and they drank it sitting on his bed. He looked at her with dark, almond-shaped eyes and took her in his arms. He was gentle and warm, and he smelled of sandalwood and spices – he smelled of home. Though gentler than Paul, he was more skilled as a lover, and she responded, thirsty for love. She cried in his arms before she slept, and in the morning, he made tea on the hot plate before they went to school.

That afternoon, the bus was running again, and she had to go home. He wanted to kiss her at the bus stop, but she thought she saw one of her neighbors and walked swiftly away from him and boarded the bus. He waited outside until it had left.

At the house, her mother-in-law complained about all the work she had had to do in Ket's absence but asked no questions, and Paul was silent as usual. Ket knew she could not continue like this. Like Madame Bovary, she would have to take poison and die a horrible death.

She found the answer on the bulletin board at school. UNRRA – the United Nations Organization for Refugees – was seeking Cambodian translators to process the refugees streaming into Thailand. She told Youn when they met at the café.

"Perhaps I could find my mother," she said, although she knew the chances were slight. "You could find your family."

They sent for applications, to be mailed to Youn's address. She helped him fill out the long form – her French was better. They mailed them in and waited.

They never talked about what they would do if one of them were selected and not the other, but Ket knew she couldn't do without him. Every day now, they skipped the café and went straight to his room and made love on his narrow bed in the short time they had before her bus. One day, when she returned home, her mother-in-law looked unusually stern.

"You are bringing disgrace on my family. You have been seen with a ..." She curled her lip in apparent disgust, unable to enunciate the word.
"*Un Cambodien?*" countered Ket. "One of my colleagues at the center. I help him with French."

But from then on, she didn't let Youn accompany her to the bus stop, and she counted the days until they would hear about their applications. She lived in dread that Paul would overcome his inhibitions and try to make love to her. The idea of his pale flesh on hers made her shudder.

Finally, when they returned to Youn's room one afternoon, they found two thick envelopes pushed under the door. They were invited to come to Geneva for a four-week training course, after which they would be sent to work in the refugee camps on the Thai-Cambodian border.

On the day they were to leave, she tried to act as if everything was as usual, that she was just going to the school and could return that evening. She took extra pains with Paul's breakfast. After all, she owed her survival to him. And he had been kind, at least at first, even letting her send money to her mother before the lines of communication were cut. She couldn't pack a suitcase, but she wore all the clothes she could, under her wool coat.

She went right from her bus to the railroad station, where Youn was waiting with the tickets. They would change in Paris for Geneva.

In the compartment, she wiped the steamy fog from the train window and looked out at the blossoms beginning to push out of the bare limbs of the apple trees. But a cold, biting rain was bearing down on them, sending them to the ground, like snowflakes. Even in the overheated train, she shivered. In Cambodia, she remembered, the brief, intermittent mango rains were just beginning, pushing the fruit to ripeness. She took off her coat and laid her head on Youn's shoulder. Through his threadbare sweater, she could hear his heart beating.

"We're going home," he said, and when he put his arm around her, she knew she was halfway there.

Je Reviens

From Julia's journal – I always imagined I would see Hourani again – maybe at one of the UN functions we sometimes attended before we moved out of the city to Westchester. I used to rehearse what I'd say, how I'd act. I wondered if I'd feel any trace of the emotion – the physical jolt -- I felt when I fell in love, or what I thought was love, with him. But we never saw each other again. People always say it's a small world – but they're wrong.

The café on the Boulevard Raspail was midway between his Metro station and the apartment, and Charles Hourani stopped there for an aperitif almost every afternoon on his way home. Today, since Denise was working the flight from Paris to Hong Kong and would not come home until the next afternoon, he had lingered longer than usual. He was sitting in his habitual place, at a small table near the wall, away from the busy street. He had read everything he wanted to read in *Le Monde*. He signaled to the old waiter to bring a second Cinzano, and then he saw them.

It was late October, and the hordes of tourists who crowded the city in summer had largely left, so Americans stood out – and few ventured this far from the standard tourist attractions. It had been, what? Fifteen years. But he recognized her at once. Julia. She had aged well. Her body was still slender, and her golden hair – which had first attracted him (though its sometimes disheveled state had irritated him) – had faded only a little and was a well-coiffed ash blonde. The man, her husband, surely, was well-dressed, not heavy but of a substantial girth. Hourani had heard she had taken up with a journalist, but this man looked too prosperous to be a reporter, more like a businessman. Between them was a child, a daughter.

He would have liked to have a daughter, a pretty little girl like this one, or a boy, a son, his son. But Denise had not wanted children. She would lose her job, she always pointed out whenever he raised the question.

"Try to imagine a pregnant stewardess?" she said. "And who would babysit? You?"

The family took a table at the edge of the sidewalk, and Hourani raised his newspaper in front of his face so he could watch them unobserved. She spoke in French to the waiter, and he smiled to himself – she still had that pronounced, but quite charming, accent. He even caught a faint whiff of the perfume she always wore. What was it called? *Je Reviens* ... that was it. But maybe it was just his imagination, a memory of the past stealing back. He had had the courier bring a bottle of it from Paris to surprise her on her birthday, he remembered. He had taken her to dinner at the excellent airport restaurant, and afterward, they had waited on the tarmac in the dark for the plane to land.

Then he remembered the way Julia looked that last day at the airport, when he left on his round-the-world trip. So lovely, so young, so sad. He had wanted to rush down the stairway and take her in his arms. But, of course, that was impossible. Still, on the too many lonely nights he had spent in hotel rooms, the image of her, putting her hands together in front of her heart in the Hindu gesture of farewell, had come back to him.

Should he go over to their table?

No, she probably wouldn't even remember him. But he had been her first lover. Women always remembered their first lovers. And even though there had been many, many women before and since, he had not forgotten her. She had been quite passionate, once he had broken through the reserve. Too passionate, too possessive – that had been why he broke it off. Denise, for all her outward warmth and emotion, was a realist –a rather hard-hearted one, he had learned.

When he returned to Phnom Penh after his long trip, Julia had gone, and Denise was waiting. He was tired of solitude, and he and Denise were married, in the cathedral at Phnom Penh, with all the diplomatic corps and even some of the royal family in attendance. Then a new man became Foreign Minister in Rabat – a devout Muslim who didn't approved of foreign wives. Or French grandmothers.

He left the diplomatic service, and through an uncle, found a job with Royal Air Maroc, which sent him first to Rome, now to Paris, as manager of the office. And Denise became a stewardess for Air France. Perhaps he should have stayed in the diplomatic service. The political winds had shifted again, and he might have been an ambassador by now, though probably in some third-world backwater, and Denise loved Paris.

The family was leaving. The husband had his hand in the air, and was calling for "*l'addition, s'il vous plait*," in the loud voice Americans use when they try to speak a foreign language.

Hourani downed his Cinzano. If he wanted to speak to her, he must act now. He started to rise, then sat down quickly and shielded his face with the newspaper. He remembered he was wearing his red Royal Air Maroc jacket. He hated wearing it, but they insisted. He looked like a clerk, especially compared to the man – Julia's husband – who was wearing what looked like a custom-tailored suit. He should have worn a topcoat. It was getting quite cold in Paris, and the jacket would have been covered. He thought nostalgically of the tropical torpor of Rio and Phnom Penh and other places where he had been posted in the diplomatic service.

He looked over the top of the newspaper and watched them leave. They were talking among themselves, and the husband held a map. He overheard the words "Montparnasse" and "Sartre." They were probably going to Sartre's grave in Montparnasse Cemetery – a popular destination for Americans of a certain age and class. They'd better hurry – the gates would soon close.

He put some coins in the saucer and folded up the newspaper. As he left the café, with its overhead heaters, he shivered and turned up the collar of his jacket. Even Rabat, with the winds off the Atlantic, was warmer than Paris. Perhaps he should have gone to work in the Ministry there. But Denise loved Paris. He shrugged.

Taking care to go in the opposite direction that Julia's family had taken, he turned into the rue du Bac. The sky was leaden, and the plane trees that lined the street had already lost most of their leaves, which swirled in the chill wind. The sidewalks were crowded with people rushing home for dinner. He felt a pang of envy, of loneliness, remembering that Denise was away.

He would go back only to change his clothes, he decided, and then go out. He didn't want to spend the evening alone.

It had started to rain, slowly at first. Reaching in his pocket, he pulled out a worn leather address book, one he had had for a long time in many cities, many countries. The ink was fading on many of the entries. Julia's address on the Rue Pasteur. Denise's where she had lived with her family, on the Boulevard Norodom.

Ah, but here, in darker ink, was Martine's phone number. Perhaps he would call Martine. Or maybe Danielle. He hadn't seen Danielle in a long, long time. A raindrop fell on the opened book, but the number was still legible. He put the book back in his pocket.

Smiling to himself, he quickened his step and walked on in the strengthening rain, the cold, gray rain of a Paris fall.

End Notes and Ephemera

When mango season is over, Julia, bereft, goes to the market and buys sheets of the preserved fruit. It tastes dry and bitter, the corpse of the once succulent fruit.

When she asks her new boyesse her name, Lanh stammers: Mademoiselle must call me "Thi Hy." It means "second sister." But Julia thought this was too impersonal and pressed till she learned her real name. But was she breaking some unwritten rule by being too intimate?

Mary leading a baby ocelot on a leash attached to a bejeweled collar. Sniffs Sheila: "She's even more exotic that he is."

General Edwards, "le celebataire geographique," swanning around in his Bermuda shorts uniform, always carrying a swagger stick.

Julia playing tennis at the Cercle Sportif early in the morning, hiring both a ball boy and an entraineur, a coach.

Jake to Julia: "For me, not having a religion is like you feel about people who don't want to swim, don't like the feel of water on their bodies."

Most of the fishermen in Cambodia were Muslim Chams, relics of the ancient kingdom of Champa, but there were a few Buddhists. They didn't take the fish's life, they claimed. The took the fish out of the water and it was so unhappy it committed suicide.

Ang Khen warning Julia not to swim out too far "for there are Thai submarines lying in wait just off the coast."

Annie Fronton's advice to Elaine: "If faut toujours être aimée plus qu'on n'aime pas." One must always be loved more than one loves. Julia's shock when Annie leaves Phnom Penh to join a Buddhist nunnery in the mountains near Ratanakiri.

The head archeologist on the bats flying out of Angkor Wat at dusk: "As if one generation of priests is banishing another."

Harper, as we prepare press material on LBJ, remembering: "He came to Manila when he was vice president and was put up at Macapagal Palace. He imperiously woke the President of the Philippines in the middle of the night, complaining that his air conditioner was too noisy."

The old French professor who hung out in the lobby of the Hotel Mondial and insisted on kissing every woman's hand. Julia shuddering at the memory of the food particles clinging to his straggly beard.

The sickly-sweet smell of bat dung mixing with the incense in the temples at Angkor. The bats flying out of the dark recesses at dusk to hunt for food, black silhouettes against the setting sun.

Ang Khem: "Paris n'est pas fait dans un jour." Paris was not built in a day.

Elaine going to a wedding of a colleague on Churi Changwar, riding in a caleche from the ferry landing to the modest paillote of the bride's family, sitting down to a meal of meat, trying to ignore the flies that landed on her plate.

On the terrace of the Continental, Julia waits for Peter. An American soldier politely offers to buy her a drink. As P. appears, the soldier stammers: "I'm sorry, ma'am." Peter saying later: "Now we've made love at the Royale and the Continental, two of the grand hotels of Indochina. Next you'll have to come to Vientiane, so we can make love at the Constellation and complete the trio."

The Indian money changer dispensing black market currency from his room atop a bookstore on Tu Do Street in Saigon.

Elaine delivering books to a political dissident under house arrest in Djakarta: the poignancy of his worn carpet slippers, as if he would never again need other footwear.

The Hotel Des Indes: a gracious columned outdoor dining pavilion in downtown Djakarta. Sukarno was heard to call it a "colonialist relic," so the owners changed the name to the Hotel Duta Indonesia—"the hotel of the Indonesian people." That way they could still use the old linens and silver with the monogram:HDI.,

The all-night wayang gulit shadow play in a field near Jogajakarta, the audience groggy as the puppeteer drones the tale of the Mahabarata, drinking sweet tea as the sun rises and good triumphs over evil.

Elaine, staying overnight at a government bungalow in rural India and being asked "For dinner, do you want vegetarian or non-vegetarian curry?" When she replies "non-vegetarian" she is told: "Sorry, we have only vegetarian." Later, in Benares and tired of the food at the ashram, she follows her nose to what she hopes is a barbecue restaurant, only to arrive, horrified, at the ghats, where bodies were burned.

Acknowledgements

Thanks to Lauren Haynes, Matthew Steinhafel, and the staff of Galaxy Galloper Press, who whipped this book into shape. Merci beaucoup to Karin Kinney, who corrected my bad French. Early readers gave me valuable advice. They include Janice Delaney, Tim Holland, Teresa Ridgeway, Tim Seldes,Susan Richards Shreve, Tim Wendel, and Hilma Wolitzer. Many friends, including Millie Boucher, Jack Golden, Roy Haverkamp, and Max Kraus, told me stories that I incorporated into the book in altered form. And last but not least, thanks to my husband, Ralph Oman, for his love and support --- as well as his copyright expertise.

MANGO RAINS

ANNE H. OMAN

MANGO RAINS

CPSIA information can be obtained
at www.ICGtesting.com
Printed in the USA
FSHW011335260120
66307FS